COMPROMISED (ALIAS PRIVATE WITNESS SECURITY ROMANCE #5)

A MM Forbidden Romantic Suspense

LISA HUGHEY

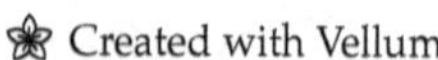 Created with Vellum

Love is love.

Chapter 1

Sasha Loblaw listened to his superior speak and imagined squeezing the life out of him, delighting as the ambassador gasped for air and clawed at the fingers wrapped around his neck, rejoicing as his face turned increasingly purple and his eyes bulged, celebrating when he went limp and his body excreted waste on the one million ruble Persian carpet and filled the rarified air of the ambassador's extravagant personal sitting room with the commonly foul stench of death.

In death, no one escaped physiological side effects. Not even the obscenely wealthy.

He continued with his fantasy. Just in case he was only mostly dead, Sasha would snap the man's neck in a gesture of joyous overkill. Then Sasha would be free.

He could physically do it right now. His fingers burned with the buzz to utilize the skills he'd been trained to use since he was a teen. But that would mess up his plans.

Instead, he listened to his boss drone on.

Boris Dubov, the Russian Ambassador to the United States,

was dressed impeccably in a custom-tailored suit that fit perfectly. He projected an air of money and power as he poured *zavarka* from the nineteenth-century, silver Nicholls & Plincke teapot, rather than a traditional samovar. He had a smooth smile and a soft handshake, his demeanor benign. One might assume he was harmless.

They would be wrong.

Sasha wore custom tailored suits designed to be slightly too big for his frame. His barely leashed raw physical power was nothing less than brutish. No one would believe he was a good guy.

They would be right.

He finally tuned back into what his boss was speaking about.

"You're going to stay in the United States while I return to *Moskva*." The ambassador displayed an arrogance that bordered on insolent. The man had never treated him as an equal, but today there was a measure of disrespect that set Sasha's finely honed instincts humming.

Had he ever noticed how arrogant the man was before now? Of course he had. But he'd chalked it up to the man's pedigree and position, and Sasha's own penchant for obediently following orders and ignoring the condescending attitude. It was not his place to question the delivery or the orders. It was strictly his place to *comply*.

Sasha tightened his muscles, hiding the rage bubbling inside him, growing stronger and more significant with the ambassador's indifferent disregard for Sasha's feelings. As if he were an animal or a lesser being because of his position. His chest pulsed with an incandescent throb. He held that fury inside and kept his face impassive.

However, he was curious. "Why?"

Why limit his access to Moscow *now*? Why keep him from returning to Russia? Was it a ploy to keep him in the United States?

It didn't really matter. He had no one to go home to. His mama had died six months ago. He'd been denied the chance to see her before she passed from a rare form of cancer.

"We have a traitor."

Sasha's heart stopped.

"Someone is feeding the Americans intelligence." The ambassador sipped the tea with a prissy affected demeanor, one pinky lifted. He'd given in to his need for a dramatic pause.

Sasha waited for him to finish. He knew the ambassador's foibles and he couldn't maintain his silence long.

Sasha had worked for Dubov for fifteen years. Done his dirty work, protected his ass, even taken a bullet for him once. But they were not friends.

Assassins didn't have friends. Bullies, enforcers, didn't have friends. They had comrades and bosses. Attachments were not allowed. Connections, to the mafia or to local government officials, that could be utilized were encouraged, but anything else was considered an indulgence and a liability. Sasha had taken that to heart, and he had had no one, except his mother.

He had been the most loyal, the most obedient soldier. He always followed orders, always did what was expected of him. He'd understood at an early age that his only way out of devastating poverty, the only way to rise into the noble class, to rise above his station, was to work for the FSB. To become their puppet. To subjugate his softer, more sensitive side in the name of defending and protecting Mother Russia.

And he'd done it.

To protect his own mother.

He'd become the brutal enforcer and assassin they had demanded he be. He'd protected his mother, given her a life of not outright luxury, but one of comfort and ease.

"Our leader wants you to suss out the traitor."

They didn't know what they asked. Or did they?

The ambassador eyed him speculatively. What was he waiting for? In all his years, Sasha had only lost it once. *Once.* When he'd been told his mother had died. Since then, he'd been the perfect Russian loyalist. The perfect employee.

The ambassador placed the ornate teapot back on the fancy wood inlay cabinet. The furniture had come from eighteenth century France and cost more than Sasha made in a month.

Before indulging in the expensive beverage, Sasha waited until the ambassador sipped more of his tea, satisfied that it was not poisoned. He drank deeply, holding the Farm Palace Imperial porcelain cup, lavishly decorated with gilt, by its delicate handle. He might be concerned—after all, doctored tea was how they killed Litvinenko. Although, Litvinenko's radioactive tea had sickened those around him as well. The ambassador would not risk himself and he had poured both their tea from the same pot.

Sasha had never questioned his orders, and even though he knew that altering his pattern of behavior was a red flag, the words burst from him. "Why me?"

"You have no one at home to return to," the ambassador replied callously. "And this will prove your loyalty."

Sasha's mouth tightened. "My loyalty has always been absolute." He'd always done what he'd been asked. No matter the consequences. "Is there some question?"

The ambassador didn't answer. Instead, he said, "You will find this traitor and we will take care of him." Kill orders were rarely spelled out verbally or written down.

Euphemisms and innuendo had been the cornerstones of his life. Sasha wondered, could he push the ambassador to issue an outright command? To order Sasha to murder this unidentified traitor?

Possibly. But he was cautious enough not to do anything that would give his boss a reason to question him.

"Understood?"

Sasha inclined his head. "Da."

The door to the sitting room flung open.

"Papa, papa." Dubov's teenaged son burst into the room. "Guess what? I made the school play."

"Yuri." Dubov's tone was harsh, sharp. "I am in a meeting."

Yuri's face fell.

"You can tell me later." Dubov's voice was soft as he smiled at his son. Dubov gave his son more leeway than Sasha would have expected. Yuri Dubov was his father's weakness. The ambassador had better be careful. There were those who would exploit that weakness.

"Hello, Sasha." The boy looked at him with speculation, clearly wondering why they were having a meeting at the residence rather than the embassy. He was smart, athletic, and very comfortable with US culture.

"Yuri." Sasha inclined his head.

Dubov pointed toward the door. "Out."

"Yes, sir." Yuri gave a curt bow and ran for the door. "Bye, Sasha."

Dubov shot a worried glance at his retreating son. Once the door closed, his boss headed for the well-hidden safe behind a painting of a Russian forest by Ivan Shishkin and spun the old-fashioned dial. Sasha listened to the turns and clicks while keeping his gaze firmly directed away from the ambassador. Instead, he watched the man in the ornate gold mirror on the opposite wall, trying surreptitiously to get a look at the contents of the safe.

Once Dubov had retrieved a package and shut the safe door, he made his way back to the settee where Sasha sipped his tea.

Dubov handed Sasha a file. "Give me your analysis."

Really? Sasha was the enforcer. He frequently read intelligence reports, but the ambassador didn't consult him on strategy. Although he should. Sasha had been around long enough to understand the nuances and consequences of most intelligence and espionage situations.

They had never allowed him to be involved in the planning which was in his favor now. They didn't know how his mind worked. They would underestimate his strategic abilities, because instead of utilizing his brain, they had maximized his body.

He could outsmart them all.

The file was thin. He flipped through the few sheets of paper. Sergei Polzin. He'd been killed in a shooting a few months ago in Washington, DC. The shooting had been investigated by the FSB and closed. Sasha sort of remembered the case. He hadn't been involved, and it was when his mother was dying, so his attention had been fractured.

"I thought this investigation had been closed."

"The US Congress is potentially going to have hearings on the matter." The ambassador shrugged. "The FSB wants it reopened. There is speculation that the traitor and Sergei are connected. We need to make sure that we are covered."

"Did we have anything to do with his death?"

"Nyet."

Because if Polzin was a traitor to Russia, the FSB would have eliminated him. Sasha considered all the angles.

"But there was more to the incident than what is public record."

No shit. There was more to every incident than the public record. All too often the public record had no bearing on what really happened.

Sasha read through the file again, struggling to pull out any other details from his memories. "Any other directions?"

"Viktor Kuznets is a person of interest."

Kuznets. "Who is he? Russian?"

His boss looked as if he'd swallowed a bad batch of caviar. "His parents defected many years ago."

The parents. Not the son. "Any other intelligence?"

"He is estranged from his family." The ambassador eyed him steadily. "Start with him."

Sasha raised a brow. Estranged. This Viktor Kuznets disagreed with his parents. If there was a rift with his parents, he'd be more likely to spy *for* Russia not against.

And how would Kuznets have gained access to Russian intelligence? And how would he be feeding it to the Americans? None of this request made sense.

"There is a picture." The ambassador gestured to the file.

Sasha flipped to the last page of the report and there was a candid photo. His heart lurched. The smiling man wore aviator glasses. He had a smooth, elegant jawline, stark cheekbones, and a high forehead with blond hair brushed away from his face. Sasha didn't have the luxury of a type, but if he had one, this man would embody it. Viktor Kuznets had the face of an angel.

An angel of doom.

Because if anyone ever figured out Sasha was attracted to him—to men—his life would be over. Maybe that's what this was all about. They were setting Sasha up for "retirement."

They wanted him to follow Kuznets. Was that it? "Observation? Kidnap? Interrogation?" Assassination?

"Observation only." The ambassador shook his head. "He works for an organization that has been in the news lately. It is also the location where Sergei Polzin was killed. Perhaps he knows more about what happened and shared it with the Americans. At this point, we just don't know."

Okay, that made more sense. But still.

"There is something unusual going on at this Adams-Larsen. It is supposedly a public relations firm. But we believe it is more." The ambassador steepled his fingers and studied Sasha as if expecting him to question the orders.

Sasha waited. Dubov couldn't outlast him. The idea was laughable. But why did the ambassador think he needed to?

Something was off about this request. If he were paranoid, he'd think the FSB wanted to watch him. That *they* were surveilling *him*.

The ambassador finally continued. "Report in daily."

Sasha didn't show his surprise, but that was also an unusual request. Typically, he was given an assignment and reported back when it was complete.

"Instructions when I find the traitor?" He did not let any uncertainty creep into his voice. But he knew he wouldn't find the traitor.

Perhaps this Viktor Kuznets would become a patsy. The traitor that he needed to find.

What would he do if they insisted that he kill Kuznets, the traitor that they were searching for? He would deal with that possibility if it arose.

"Depends on who it is." The true nature of the ambassador was revealed in his cold dead eyes and grim mouth. "Once they are uncovered, we will deal with them punitively. Permanently."

Death. Sasha was tired of killing. His motherland, Russia, no longer held any sway over him. Perhaps, even though he didn't believe he had given away his feelings, they could sense his disgust for this life. And for them.

He was done being used. Sasha would pretend to search for this traitor.

And then he would disappear.

———————————————

Chapter 2

———————————————

*V*iktor Kuznets was done. Done with secrets. Done with trying to be perfect.

He couldn't imagine life getting any better. He had finally found his place in the world. Acceptance and belonging curled around him like a blanket of happiness.

He'd almost fucked it all up when he'd inadvertently put his friends in danger after hooking up with the wrong guy. But his friends had understood his mistake, and instead of cutting him out, gave him forgiveness.

He would never again do anything to destroy the trust they'd placed in him.

For years he'd tried so hard to be perfect. To do anything that was asked of him. To do nothing that would jeopardize his place. Turned out all he'd really needed to do was be human. His screw up had granted the entry he hadn't been able to find in perfection.

The conference room at Adams-Larsen Inc and Associates —ALIAS as they affectionately called themselves—was alive with teasing and jokes. Publicly, they were an image consulting firm. Privately, they did something altogether different.

The converted dining room of the old brownstone that housed their operations was noisy as his friends prepared for their weekly staff meeting. A plate of fluffy pastry with a drizzle of shiny syrup sat on the credenza that held the coffee and tea service.

Marsh leaned over the china plate. "Yum. What are these?"

Maria Torres, the newest member of their private witness protection and relocation team, beamed. "A recipe from that British baking show."

Kita Kim, their resident martial arts badass and social media seeder and hacker, stuffed two into her mouth. She lavished praise around the lump of pastry. "Oh my God. These are so good."

Viktor filled his plate and then took his seat at the conference table. He smiled slightly as he listened to the banter around him.

Viktor dipped his chin. *Thank you, Universe, for this food.*

He took a small, almost dainty, bite of the pastry. The sweet flaky layers melted on his tongue. He forced himself not to rush. Even after years of food security, with plenty to eat and easily accessible, it was difficult not to revert to that starving kid and gobble down the treat not knowing when he'd have his next meal. Instead, he savored slowly and enjoyed the chaos around him.

"Hey, hey." Dwayne Lameko, their Dwayne "The Rock" Johnson lookalike, swatted Kita's fingers. "Leave some for the rest of us."

"Ha. I bet you have a whole plate of these at home."

Maria and Dwayne had finally gotten together on an op and were dating exclusively. After her ordeal as a young girl, Maria was free and beginning to blossom. Viktor was so happy for her. Kita shoved another one into her mouth as Dwayne chased her around the table.

"Help me, Viktor. He hurt me!" Kita screeched. "I need medical assistance."

He was their medic. Fortunately, they hadn't needed his skills recently. And they certainly wouldn't need them this morning.

He snorted. "Better be careful or you'll choke on that second treat."

"Wow. That's cold." Kita laughed, then fist-bumped him. "Nice."

Marsh Adams, co-founder of ALIAS, was finally back in the office after being undercover and incommunicado for months. His objective had been to protect the company and their reputation, but it had turned into a secret op that ended in the apprehension of an international criminal. Marsh laughed and snatched one off the plate while Kita and Dwayne were busy bickering like siblings.

Marsh said, "Did I really miss this?"

Kita grinned at their boss. "Of course you did."

Viktor waited quietly for Jillian to appear so they could begin. Kita placed a mug of mint tea at his elbow. "See! I don't hold a grudge. Even though I could be maimed right now, by the giant," she jerked her thumb toward Dwayne, "and *you* didn't protect me."

"Give it up, Kita." Dwayne smirked. Everyone knew Dwayne would never hurt anyone smaller than him, although to be fair, everyone was smaller than him.

Not to mention Kita could kick ass.

Viktor said, "You are a strong, confident woman. I knew you could defend yourself and I was allowing you to exercise your abilities rather than taking over."

"Ha!" Kita chucked him on the shoulder. "Good recovery."

He loved these people. They had given him a home when his family had rejected him. They had forgiven him for his lapse in protocol even when he had no excuse.

Loneliness was not a reason to betray your friends. And he hadn't. *He hadn't.* But he'd been careless, and that negligent slip had almost cost their lives. Their benevolence humbled him. He would never betray their trust again. He would protect his teammates with the ferocity of a pitbull against any threat.

Jake Brown sat at the other end of the table. When Maria offered him a pastry, he smiled tightly and took one in his large, meaty hand. He had been awfully quiet lately. Viktor made a note to check in with him. Something had happened on a relocation a few months ago, and he hadn't been the same afterwards. He was never very chatty, but lately he'd been downright taciturn.

"Okay everyone. Let's get started." Marsh sat at the head of the table.

"What about Jill?" Kita plopped into the chair next to Viktor and punched him in the arm.

"She's…occupied." Marsh glanced at the stairs leading to Jill's office.

His stomach churned. They never scheduled appointments during their weekly staff meetings. Their business was more than private. It was critical that they kept their client's secrets.

"We're going to start the staff meeting while we have company?" Kita voiced the question everyone was thinking.

"General admin only at the moment." Marsh sidestepped the question.

They all nodded in agreement. ALIAS kept a lot of secrets that could have deadly consequences if someone were to overhear.

His life had been one big secret for years. First when he hid his sexuality from his parents. Then, the military. He no longer hid his sexual identity. But of course, he'd lost his parents over that. Turned out pretending he wasn't gay was what his parents had wanted. Ignoring his sexuality was better than being out.

Everyone had settled in and stopped kidding around when their new receptionist, Hannah, sauntered down the stairs. "Viktor, Jill needs to see you in her office."

Jillian Larsen, the other co-founder boss at the prestigious Adams-Larsen agency, was skipping the staff meeting and now wanted him in her office.

Could this be related to his screw up?

Because of his actions the company was under increased scrutiny by the public. Their very private witness protection and covert relocation agency was in jeopardy because of him. He had been targeted by criminals seeking confidential information about one of their clients and he'd fallen for the oldest trick in the book, because his very recent ex-boyfriend had dumped him.

Viktor had come home from an op and his apartment had been empty. Jonathon had moved out, taking all their art and most of the furniture with him.

Jonathon left because he felt like Viktor was keeping secrets…which of course he was. That's what he did. That's what ALIAS did. Viktor had known that Jonathon wasn't thrilled with his inability to share, but he'd had no idea that his boyfriend of a year was so unhappy that he'd disappear in the middle of the day—like one of their clients.

And that night at the bar, after too much rum and too much heartache, he'd said, *fuck caution,* and let a guy pick him up. Viktor had gone to a stranger's hotel room and had sex with him.

But it hadn't been random.

That miscalculation had cost him. And for what?

With the perspective of a month without his ex, Viktor realized that he'd built a fantasy life around his ex-boyfriend. He'd been in love with the idea of what he and Jonathon *could* be, not what they really were. That was still no excuse for being dumb enough to be duped.

He'd left himself, his friends, vulnerable. Perhaps Jillian had changed her mind and had decided to punish him.

He knocked sharply on Jillian Larsen's door and waited.

"Come."

Viktor pushed open the door and stopped abruptly. Jillian wasn't alone. He didn't recognize the man sitting on the settee. *What was happening?*

"Have a seat," Jill said. She had his undying gratitude for supporting him. She'd always been a little...standoffish. Which he totally understood. Revealing your vulnerability, that soft underbelly was a liability. Especially in this job.

Even more so for a woman. She couldn't be perceived as weak.

She was the big boss. But when she'd gone through her own trauma and met the love of her life, a braw Scottish law enforcement officer, she had become more relaxed. She could still be a hard ass, but Viktor understood her better now.

Viktor headed toward the grouping of seats in Jill's office, deliberately evening his stride.

"Our associate has a proposition for you."

Viktor raised one eyebrow. Associate? Proposition? *Way to be vague, boss.*

He sat on the least obvious choice, a dainty wing chair that barely accommodated his bulk. "What can I do for you?"

"I'm glad you asked." The man's vocal cords were gravelly with years of smoking. The stench of cigarettes wafted from his clothing and gave away his vice. No one introduced the man by name.

The Cigarette Man handed a photograph to Viktor. The man in the picture was attractive. Not that tall, built like a bull with wide, bulky shoulders, barrel chest, trim waist, and thick, muscular thighs. His face held an intensity that was compelling, magnetic.

If he were in a bar Viktor would look twice, maybe three times at this guy. His presence nearly leapt off the glossy photo paper.

"Do you know him?" The unnamed man asked.

Viktor studied the man in the photograph, picking out the details of his surroundings, of his clothing, of his body language. He stood in a fancy restaurant, one table away from a group of men in suits who were eating and drinking, while his sharp eyes studied the surroundings.

Confidence oozed from him. The suit was custom made, expensive, his stance seemingly casual, but there was an alertness to his gaze and his hand rested on his hip near the opening of his jacket, likely for easy access to a weapon.

The dichotomy between the expensive suit and the body of the brawler was extremely compelling.

The restaurant was expensive, exclusive, with dark wood and white linen tablecloths. Clusters of empty wine glasses and highballs grouped at each place setting. The men at the table were laughing and gesturing. Servers hovered a few tables away, clearly on standby for the moment the men needed anything, but far enough away that they couldn't overhear the conversation. The man was a bodyguard or security for wealthy patrons.

The men he was keeping safe were Slavic. Russian, maybe Ukrainian, or one of the Stans. The Eastern European men seemed at ease with the bodyguards around them and expected deferential restaurant service. The privilege was evident in the cant of their heads and the way they ignored everyone but the other men at the table.

"I don't believe so."

"His name is Sasha Loblaw. He's an agent of the FSB and we want to turn him."

The FSB, *Federalnaya Sluzhba Bezopasnosti*, the Russian Federal Security Service, was the modern day KGB. Their director reported directly to Putin.

Okay, but what did that have to do with Viktor? And who was *we*? That information seemed exceedingly sensitive to share with him. Viktor's high-level, top-secret clearance had been revoked when he left his job with the military and the CIA. So why was this unnamed man sitting in Jill's office sharing an intelligence target?

Viktor stayed silent, waiting for the man to explain.

"We'd like you to…get close to him."

None of that cryptic bullshit. This guy was going to have to spell out exactly what he wanted. "Get close to him…and?"

The man stayed silent.

Viktor wouldn't be the first to break. He stared steadily at the man until Cigarette Man shifted his gaze. "We'd like some compromising pictures."

Sickness roiled in his stomach. He knew what the guy was asking. Basically, he wanted Viktor to do to this Sasha what had been done to him. Lie and get close to the man. Which was code for have sex with him. While he found Sasha Loblaw attractive, he hadn't sold his body for his adopted country…yet.

This man and whatever agency he worked for, wanted dirt on a target and they were willing to use any means or anyone to get it. He knew that was how the game was played. But Viktor was tired of being a pawn.

As if he read Viktor's mind, the man said, "You don't have to have sex with him. Unless you want to." The guy wheezed out a laugh as if he'd said something funny. "We just need some kompromat to persuade him that working for us in his best interests."

Viktor's gaze shot to Jill.

I'm sorry, she mouthed.

His tension eased. She hadn't known that was what the guy was going to ask.

"Why me?" Because they both liked dick? Presumably this Sasha Loblaw was gay. However, it paid never to assume anything.

"Because of the connection to Russia."

Viktor blinked. He no longer had a connection to Russia. His parents had defected years ago.

He hadn't been back to Russia since they had snuck away in the middle of the night. He had no love for his birth country. He also didn't have a desire to deceive this Sasha Loblaw.

But he wasn't going to argue with this guy, because there was a reason Cigarette Man was in Jill's office going through semi-official means, instead of approaching Viktor outside of ALIAS. So he kept his mouth shut and waited.

"We've planted some rumors about Sergei Polzin in the hopes that Loblaw and the Kremlin will bite."

"What kind of rumors?"

"The kind that will get them to reopen the investigation into Sergei's death."

That would be bad for ALIAS since the man had been killed here. That was an unfortunate fact. Adams-Larsen had sheltered a woman running from the Russian in their safe room and Sergei had found her here. When Sergei opened fire, they'd had no choice but to shoot to kill. To protect the victims hiding from Polzin.

"We've planted intelligence that will cause them to focus on you."

So…bait. And based on what Cigarette Man had just said, they had already set things up.

They wanted Viktor to be a target for Sasha Loblaw.

"What is in it for me?" Viktor asked.

"As you're aware, there are some rumors swirling inside the Beltway about Adams-Larsen. Especially after the shooting of Sergei." The guy smoothed a hand over his knee. He leaned back against the settee, his ankle rested on the opposite knee, creating a triangle between his legs as he bobbed his shiny wingtip shoe. Was he nervous or just generally fidgety? The white man was dressed neat as a pin, perfectly combed hair, clean fingernails, and a bland demeanor. But his shiny left shoe had one scuff mark near the ball of his foot. Was that on purpose? Was he trying to appear a little sloppy so he'd be underestimated, or was he actually a little sloppy? "And then of course, the recent trouble."

Trouble he'd precipitated by being a dumbass. Finally, Viktor asked, "Why would I do that?"

"Let's just say I can make life easier for your boss, and your company, if you help us out."

Great, blackmail. The inference was that he could also make things worse for ALIAS.

Viktor's stomach roiled.

The setup turned Viktor's stomach. But there had been a new article in the *Post* about ALIAS and unless there was some fancy shielding or misdirection, the press was going to keep searching for information about what ALIAS really did.

Viktor didn't trust this guy. He waited because he was certain there was more. He was correct.

"I have access to his schedule. He frequents a bar in DC regularly." The Cigarette Man continued as if it was a done deal. "According to an informant, he has orders to investigate ALIAS over the holidays."

"So while he is investigating ALIAS, I'm supposed to lure him in," with his charming personality aka potential sexual favors, "and get him in a compromising position?" His distaste for the job was evident in his tone.

Jill had been completely silent.

"That is the plan."

One that had been conceived and partially executed before they'd even gotten Viktor's cooperation. Because they knew ALIAS had problems.

Those rumors swirling about…he'd helped cause them and if this would fix it then he was all in. Whether he wanted to be or not.

"What do I have to do?"

Chapter 3

*V*iktor hated lying.

But if that was what he had to do to protect ALIAS and his friends: go undercover, leave himself open to connecting with Sasha Loblaw, and set the guy up for some compromising photos, then he would do it. Even if it left a bad taste in his mouth.

The best way to lie was to incorporate some element of truth into the lie. He figured that his attraction to Sasha Loblaw would be the truth.

Before he approached Sasha, he planned to do some reconnaissance.

Viktor sat at the bar in the luxury hotel that catered to foreign dignitaries, and where the Russian consulate housed visiting diplomats and vaunted guests who were connected to the Kremlin.

Viktor struck a seemingly casual pose and stroked his middle finger up and down the shot glass of high-end Grey Goose, ostensibly studying the colorless liquid. He surreptitiously observed the occupants of the bar in the reflection of the mirror wall behind the various top-shelf bottles of liquor.

He hated vodka, so it was easy to ignore the drink.

The décor was what Viktor called "Ancient Washington Elite" with lots of dark, wainscoting paneling, rich tapestries on the walls, and large plush chairs. Even the bar stools were heavy wood with claw feet and arms upholstered in heavy brocade. The ornate mahogany bar was long and curved.

The paintings on the walls were originals of hunting parties and pastoral manors, as if this were an eighteenth-century English country house and not a modern hotel.

Viktor watched the murky reflections of the other patrons. It was crowded for a random weeknight in late December. Congress was out of session and most elected officials were back in their home states to celebrate the holidays with their families. Diplomats had returned to their own countries until after the new year. Typically, not much went on in the capital during the holidays.

Normally, a plethora of movers and shakers congregated here to trade gossip and make deals. The location seemed far too public to Viktor, but Sasha Loblaw apparently frequented this hotel bar twice a week. The regular schedule seemed odd to Viktor. Unless there was tradecraft going on and this was a dead drop location. That also seemed unlikely. However, it paid to keep an open mind and watchful eye.

Could he have seen Sasha Loblaw here before? Maybe he had and didn't remember. He and Jonathon had come here regularly when they'd been living together. Fortunately, he didn't have to worry about running into his ex. Jonathon spent the holidays in Florida with his parents.

Sasha Loblaw was the head of security for the Russian Embassy in Washington and rumored to be the highest-ranking FSB officer in the US. He provided security for the current ambassador, Boris Dubov, and his family. Officially, Sasha spent his time attending meetings at the embassy and doing advance security scouting before any offsite meetings.

Unofficially, he was a rumored assassin.

All information the Cigarette Man had neglected to share with Viktor. Fortunately, he knew better than to trust a government guy who was basically blackmailing him and he knew how to do his own damn research so that he went into a situation armed with facts.

Viktor's target sauntered into the bar.

Sasha Loblaw was compelling in that rough and raw way. Blunt features, a nose too big for his face and ruddy cheekbones which could be a function of the frigid December night—or the result of an excessive love of vodka or love for an *excess* of vodka. His sexuality was like a punch to the face and Viktor's body responded to those pheromones before he could suppress his reaction.

Damn. In person, the man's sex appeal was magnified times a million. Loblaw's sheer presence had not come through in that glossy photo. He had never run into Sasha. He definitely would have remembered.

Sasha was the exact opposite of the kind of guy Viktor normally found attractive. His boyfriends had all been charming, elegant, refined, and cultured. They favored art galleries and wine tastings, not gun ranges and beer fests.

Loblaw was not charming.

Sasha exuded violence and sex. He was gruff, blunt, like a bull in a pen full of cows, except Viktor assumed that Sasha preferred other bulls—although in the few pictures that Viktor had tracked down of the man, he'd been working and not with anyone, male or female. That lack of female companionship was why Viktor believed he had been handpicked for this job. Their commonality wasn't Russia—it was men.

Nothing about the guy was subtle.

The public information on Sasha Loblaw was shockingly scarce. Even for Russia, which was notorious for being close-mouthed about the personal information of their state employees. These days it was nearly impossible to hide with social media and the multitude of ways that people on the internet could be tracked.

Single, never married. There were only a few photographs of him, mostly partials of his face; he'd somehow always turned away from the camera and yet still managed to put his body between any threat and the ambassador.

A protector. But natural or bred? Would he protect himself if he knew that he was being threatened?

Sasha muscled his way through two-thousand-dollar suits and four-hundred-dollar haircuts, swaggering up to the bar with a confidence that wasn't misplaced. Every gay guy in the bar was checking him out.

Shit. Viktor was in serious trouble.

No way would this guy believe that Viktor was randomly at his favorite bar. He should have let Sasha find him. But he'd wanted to control their initial meet. Tonight was off the books. Mostly reconnaissance. He hadn't let Cigarette Man or Jill know of his plans. It should be fine. A man like Sasha would do research before he hooked up with someone. No way would he bite on the first meet.

Everything about this assignment felt out of control. Picking the time and location of their initial interaction was the one area where he could have some influence. *That was a mistake.*

Viktor was without backup, because the only other person at ALIAS who knew about the situation was Jill. He left her out of this plan because he'd already caused enough blowback on the company. But he knew if he needed her, she would drop everything to help him.

"You aren't required to sleep with him." Jillian had made that abundantly clear after the Cigarette Man had left. Sex wasn't part of this op. But if Sasha was interested, Viktor would take one for the team. Because that was what he needed to do to atone, even if it filled him with self-loathing.

The bartender—Mike, Mick, Mack, something—gave Viktor a sexy smile and a very unsubtle eye fuck. "Haven't seen you here in a while." Mick—no, *Mack*—smiled. "Holidays keeping you busy?"

Not really. Viktor shrugged. "Life has been…complicated."

He was hyper aware of the moment Sasha swaggered over to the bar and ordered. "Two cosmopolitans."

Unexpected. The slightly girly drink made Viktor want to smile. Instead, he kept his expression bland, as if he hadn't noticed that Sasha was standing right next to him.

The bartender gave Sasha a once over and nodded. "Coming right up."

"You going to continue to ignore me?"

Viktor couldn't see who Sasha was talking to. He'd let his over long hair flop in his eyes and now his intel was lacking.

Until Sasha nudged him with his elbow. Viktor turned to look at the man, surprised at the unexpected touch. Sasha raised a brow and waited.

Viktor straightened from his slouch and tossed the hair from his gaze. "You talking to me?"

Sasha looked past Viktor at the wall behind him. He'd chosen the stool at the corner of the bar and the wall so he'd have a good view of the entire room, and no one could sneak up on him.

Sasha sat next to him. "Da."

Viktor blinked again. Surprising.

He scanned the bar quickly looking for Sasha's backup, but he didn't tag anyone else in the upscale bar. That didn't mean they didn't exist and weren't watching, but if he had it, Sasha's backup was well hidden.

Maybe he was working solo.

Like Viktor.

Viktor returned his gaze to Sasha. Goddamn, he was hot. Like DC in July or Chernobyl after the meltdown. He could light a guy on fire with his presence.

"*Na Zdorovie.*" Viktor lifted his shot glass and toasted, a welcome and a warning. He tossed back the Grey Goose and let the familiar burn of alcohol burn through him. Then Viktor took a chance. "I hear you're looking for me."

Sasha raised an eyebrow. "I'm looking for answers and I think you can give them to me."

Viktor set down his shot glass and leaned in close to his salvation and his enemy. "I can give you lots of things."

Viktor had pegged Sasha as closeted. If the Russian government knew that he was gay, it could be a death sentence. The official FSB stance on homosexuality was that it wasn't illegal; however, the law provided no protections for LGBTQ+ citizens. The FSB, which built their reputation on ways to develop compromising intelligence on their enemies, couldn't afford to have an agent who was gay. He hoped they never found out Sasha Loblaw was gay.

Viktor would hate for this man to "accidently fall in front of a train." He was…magnificent.

Except if Cigarette Man had his way, they would use Viktor to hurt him. *Fuck.*

A small smile quirked Sasha's lush mouth at Viktor's innuendo. "That's very provocative, but I don't—how do Americans put it?—swing that way."

Lie.

Viktor didn't have concrete intelligence that refuted that statement, but he swore he could feel it from the very potent pheromones Sasha emitted.

He decided to push. "Ever thought of…experimenting?"

Sasha's nostrils flared and his pupils widened. "Not at present." His words were clipped.

Viktor thought he heard a "maybe later" in there—if the banked heat in the guy's icy gray gaze was any indication, later might just happen.

His cock rose at the idea of having this man in bed. Pressed up against him bare chest to bare muscled chest, Sasha's hard cock in Viktor's hand and Sasha's mouth brutalizing his in the most erotic way.

As if he'd seen a ghost, Sasha's expression went blank, his eyes turned cold, and his mouth flattened. Whatever he thought he'd seen in Sasha's eyes was gone.

"Pity." Viktor smiled. "Let's get down to business."

"Sergei Polzin," Sasha replied.

The game was on.

Chapter 4

*S*asha Loblaw was tired of his life.

Tired of the machinations, the lies, and never being able to trust anyone.

Viktor Kuznets was lying to him right now. They would do this dance until Sasha got the information he needed, and then he would move on. As he always did.

The ambassador had told Sasha to find a suspected double agent in Washington and then given him Viktor's name.

The request to start with Kuznets had been blunt with little nuance.

According to his intel, Viktor's only allegiance was to his employer: Adams-Larsen Inc and Associates. A PR firm that had nothing to do with PR. If his sources were correct, Adams-Larsen was about to be summarily outed in the press.

Rumor on the Hill was that they did private witness security and made people disappear. For safety reasons. Not "disappear" like his government disappeared people. Russia's form of "disappear" was double speak for dead and buried. Typically gruesomely dead, dismembered, blown up, fall in front of a train, or poisoned by a new chemical weapon made to mimic illness.

Then buried or weighted down and dropped in the Potomac.

Sasha knew Viktor wasn't the double agent they were looking for, but he needed to meet with him and go through the motions. As far as Sasha could discern, the guy wasn't even a single agent. Sasha found no evidence that Viktor worked for anyone in either the US or Russian government. He couldn't fathom how he might be selling Russian secrets. He had made himself available like a sacrificial lamb.

He needed to figure out why his superiors had put Viktor in his path.

Were they trying to tempt him? Were they trying to trap him? Or was he jumping at shadows that didn't exist? He just didn't know.

He was being watched. He'd seen the tails over the last few weeks. Rather than evade them, he just let them follow and developed files on every operative who had been watching him. Men he'd trained were now following him as if he were the enemy.

When he needed to move in secrecy, he took precautions and obscured his routes. He scanned his home and office regularly for listening devices and made sure never to say anything that would incriminate him in anyway. He'd disabled the GPS on his official cell phone. He rarely used his car, so he left their tracking device on it.

He clearly didn't have long left.

He'd lived in the United States long enough, seen firsthand the positive impact of democracy. While the US had its flaws, he no longer wanted to go home. He liked it here. Even if the bulk of the US citizens had no appreciation for the liberty and freedom they took for granted.

He had begun this life as a patriot, but he would end it as a traitor.

"What do you want to know about Sergei Polzin?" Viktor rimmed his shot glass with his index finger and gave Sasha a smoky look.

Piz-dets, he was hot. But Sasha didn't know if this was a setup. He had always been loyal to Russia. Until he hadn't. They had tested him many times. He used to just shrug it off, seen the tests as standard procedure.

But lately…it made him angry. The FSB had invested years training him, but he was getting older. Over forty, his physical body was not going to be able to beat or compete with the younger operatives. He was on the verge of being disposable. He had given years, one could argue *his best years*, to his country—never betraying their trust. Until they had betrayed him.

So, he was tired and angry. Not a great combination.

He was tired of the bullshit, and he was tired of the fight. He slapped his palm on the bar. "Is this a test?"

Viktor cocked his head and stared at him lazily, barely reacting to Sasha's outburst. "Not at all. I heard you might be looking for me and I made myself available."

"Where do your loyalties lie?"

"None of your business." Viktor bared his teeth, his smile holding a sexual edge. "I'd have to know you a whole lot better before I gave you that kind of insight."

"Everything okay here, gentleman?" The bartender had checked on them several times, trying desperately to flirt.

"We're fine," Viktor said flatly, shutting him down. "We'll signal if we need anything."

The guy's face fell. What was he thinking? They'd have a threeway?

Sasha was in here a couple of times a week. He had never

left with a man. The chippy bartender was annoying, and Sasha turned his death stare on the man.

Trained assassins had quivered in fear when he looked at them like that. The bartender was no exception. His face blanched and he scurried away.

Sasha relaxed. "There are some rumblings that Polzin had been trying to double deal on several crates of Makarov pistols."

Viktor's face betrayed no emotion, but his level of intensity ramped up. So he hadn't known that. "Funny, the rumblings I heard was that he came here to assassinate a high-level defector who was in US custody."

"Interesting." Sasha had heard that as well. As a matter of fact, as far as he knew, that had been the original intent, but he also knew that clearly something had gone off plan since Polzin was dead. "You don't know anything about the weapons?" Sasha said.

"That is not intelligence I have heard." Viktor sipped from his shot glass. Sasha found himself distracted by the purse of his lips. "However, my sources are likely different than yours."

Sasha believed him. "Any way you could confirm my information?"

Viktor set down the empty glass. "I can certainly look into it."

The exchange so far had been very civilized but under the surface a sexual tension was brewing. Viktor made Sasha wish things were different. Made him wish his life were different. Because if he'd been an average guy, and free to indulge, he'd have taken the man up on his very unsubtle offer.

"However…" Viktor lifted the martini that Sasha had bought for him, curling his fingers around the glass with a slow, sensual grasp. He stared Sasha straight in the eye. "How are you going to make that worth my while?"

He tossed back the drink and set the glass on the bar top with a thump.

Sasha knew how he would like to make it worth Viktor's while, but that was not in their cards. "I am authorized to offer you money." He had a cache of disposable money available for payoffs. Bribes and favors as currency were standard in his world.

Viktor snorted. "No, thanks."

No hesitation. Sasha wasn't surprised, and yet he was. "To be determined later." The words came out husky and, much to his dismay, with more than a hint of sexual innuendo.

Sasha had to come up with some actionable intelligence. They wanted a traitor, and he was going to have to give them one. Before meeting Viktor, Sasha had been toying with giving them Viktor. But now he didn't want to.

Viktor leaned back against the wall and let his gaze drift around the room, clearly taking in the clientele and assessing for any danger.

Sasha liked him.

"Where are you from?" Sasha wanted to know more about the intriguing Viktor. Where he lived. What he did for pleasure. What he hated. What he loved.

"Your research didn't tell you?"

Sasha shrugged. "I prefer to verify."

"I am American," Viktor declared with more than a hint of pride.

Not even a smidgeon reluctance in his answer. No way was this man in the market to become a spy. Even if he was the best liar in Washington, a gargantuan feat, it was difficult to fake that kind of resolve.

"That's it?"

"That's all that matters." Again, a ring of truth in his words.

Their banter called to Sasha. Another time, another place and maybe he would have tried to carve out a way to be with Viktor Kuznets.

Regret pulsed through him.

He should probably head home. Sasha had gotten the intel he needed, and his bosses would know that he'd met with Viktor. It was time to leave.

Yet he was reluctant. He wanted to stay. Completely inadvisable. And a recipe for questions from his superiors. But unless they had somehow bugged the bar, they wouldn't know exactly what he and Viktor were discussing.

Sasha held up two fingers and the puppy-dog bartender hustled over with two more drinks as if he was watching intently.

Viktor just smiled and raised the martini glass. "To new beginnings."

He had no idea how fucking true that statement was. "Fresh starts."

The heat emanating from Viktor could set the embassy on fire. But what really intrigued Sasha was the guardedness and sadness.

"What is your favorite American sport?" Sasha watched the Washington Wizards on the television above the bar.

"Hockey," Viktor replied. "You?"

The Wizards' new point guard dribbled circles around the front court before putting up a fade away two. "Basketball." Sasha lifted his chin toward the screen over the bar. "It's so delightfully American. Nyet?"

"Yes." Viktor turned his attention to the screen.

For a few minutes, they watched the men on the court, sweaty and physical as they crashed into each other, competing for the ball. Sasha was hyper aware of the physicality of the man next to him. He exuded a sexual energy that called to every fiber of his being. "It's very… unpredictable. They have a strategy and plans, but sometimes there's an unexpected steal or a blocked shot, and the whole game shifts."

Viktor turned so his body was perpendicular to Sasha. His legs spread wide bracketing Sasha's body. "You like games?"

"Depends on what the game is." Sasha raised his brows and lifted his fingers for another two martinis. "And who is playing."

They weren't talking about basketball anymore.

Heat rose from Viktor's body. The sexual tension between them hot enough to melt ice as they studiously avoided looking at each other.

"You play much?" Viktor asked.

The conversation had drifted into sultry, forbidden territory.

"Rarely have the time."

"Pity." Viktor licked sugar from the rim of the martini glass. Sasha's pulse kicked as he imagined that pink tongue licking him. His cock responded to the images flickering in his consciousness, of Viktor with his mouth wrapped around Sasha's cock.

Sasha's heart thundered. This man was forbidden.

He tipped his head at Viktor. "Unfortunate circumstances."

His initial idea to serve up Viktor as a sacrificial lamb was dead—the idea so distasteful it left him physically ill.

"How long are you in town?" Viktor asked.

"The situation is fluid." Until he had orders, or he figured out how he was going to get out of this mess, he was stuck in DC.

Viktor tossed back the rest of the cosmo. The muscles in his neck contracted as he swallowed. He set the martini glass down on the bar lazily. His mouth was glossy with the liquor and his eyes, a mossy green, heavy lidded with erotic suggestion.

"Surprisingly...tasty," Viktor commented.

"Sweet with a hint of bite."

"Bite is always good," Viktor shot back.

Sasha was tempted to say the hell with it and take him in the park. Except he didn't want a furtive, sullied, encounter in the dark, hidden as if there were shame in their attraction. He wanted a bed with satin sheets, vodka chilling in a bed of crushed ice, some oysters and hot sauce, and hours to explore that hard muscled body.

Sasha sighed. Those were futile daydreams that were never going to come true. But dammit he was tired of hiding.

"Tell me something about you," Sasha demanded, the liquor loosening his tongue.

Viktor understood what he meant. He didn't even prevaricate. "I like weapons."

"Why?"

"When you're young and defenseless, you feel like weapons will save you." Viktor laughed, but it wasn't with amusement. "Of course, then you grow up and realize that it's far more complicated. But that need doesn't go away."

"The best weapon is your mind," Sasha countered.

Viktor shook his head. "Coming from you...that's intriguing and likely disingenuous."

"From me?"

"I know you are proficient with weapons," Viktor said.

"I only meant that physical weapons are a known quantity. A mind is full of possibility and many, many surprises." Sasha shared more than he should have with that. "I'd best be going."

He stood up and the room fuzzed a bit. The alcohol should have been less than a blip on his metabolism. The drink loosened his tongue. "It's been a pleasure." But the words were not as crisp as he needed them to be. Soft, slightly slurred. His regret, which he needed to keep to himself, was clear.

The bartender was on the phone, but he gave Sasha a thumbs-up, letting him know he'd put the drinks on his tab.

"You okay?" Viktor frowned.

"Fine." However, the room went in and out of focus.

"Let me walk you out."

"I am not some schoolboy with his first time drinking alcohol."

"You are definitely not a boy," Viktor ground out. His pretty features blurred a little.

Something was wrong, but somehow Sasha couldn't bring himself to care. He headed into the lobby of the fancy hotel, mere steps from the White House and the Mall.

Viktor kept pace with him, but he seemed to stagger for a moment.

"An American who can't hold his vodka," Sasha teased. Except the words had been a sloppy. There was something in Viktor's gaze besides annoyance. Regret?

Sasha couldn't seem to process anything.

His thoughts were sluggish, slow, and moving his arms and legs felt like they were on strings controlled by someone else.

Sasha wanted to tell Viktor to watch his back. Be careful. Because clearly someone had targeted him. A stinging regret pierced through him, breaking through the fog.

Perhaps the motive behind his task was to assess if Viktor was a potential recruit for Russia. His time in the US Army and then his work at the Central Intelligence Agency made him an attractive possibility.

Before he could say anything else, Viktor's knees dipped,

and Sasha grabbed for him. They clung together each propping the other up.

A bench outside the entrance to the bar was tucked away on the side of the lobby. A potted palm hid the area from public view. Sasha waded through the increasing fog in his head, his only focus to get them both to the bench. He tugged Viktor into the alcove, and they collapsed onto the seat. "Let's just rest here for a moment."

He couldn't seem to process anything. His eyes drifted closed for a moment.

"I feel funny." Viktor slumped next to him.

"I don't feel anything." True. Sasha was emotionally dead. No longer a puppet for his master. He'd been set free by their disregard for his wishes regarding his mother.

"I'm sorry." Viktor leaned back against the wall.

"Me too."

In a moment of clarity, he confessed, "I like you, Viktor. I didn't expect to."

And that was it.

Chapter 5

---

*S*omeone had taken up the Russian tank drum in Viktor's brain and they wouldn't shut the fuck up. Every bang reverberated against his skull with a loud boom. Jesus, he must have had more to drink than he thought last night.

Sasha really could put it away.

He buried his head under the pillow to hide from the harsh morning light piercing his eyeballs and increasing the tempo of the drums.

His mouth tasted like death and as he ran his tongue over the fuzz covering his teeth, he wondered how he'd gotten so trashed. Again.

Jill was going to be pissed.

The drums throbbed in his head and behind his eyelids. He lay on his stomach, ultra still, not wanting to do anything to cause his head to break apart and shatter into a billion pieces. As he lay on the sheets, details registered. The silky fabric felt unfamiliar beneath his cheek. Viktor pressed his palm flat against the mattress and absorbed the texture through his fingertips.

He was naked, could feel his morning erection pressing into the mattress. Over the pounding in his head, he could smell something delicious. Unfamiliar but delicious.

He cracked open his eyelids, the blinding white caused him to scrunch them closed again. That didn't make sense. He always kept the blinds in his apartment closed. More to keep out unwanted snoopers than the sun, but the result was the same.

That small glimpse revealed an unfamiliar room. He wasn't in his own bed. Where the hell was he? What had happened?

Tentatively he opened his eyes again and, without moving, catalogued what he could see.

A hotel room? That he had no recollection of entering. He thought back to last night. He and Sasha had circled each other in a verbal game of cat and mouse that had felt more like foreplay than espionage. But he'd gotten Sasha's message loud and clear. There was no way in hell the uber-cautious Sasha was going to be trapped in a compromising situation.

Viktor contrarily realized he didn't want to put him in one. Screw the Cigarette Man. Viktor had no desire to destroy the guy's life. Assuming that Sasha wouldn't kill him if he tried.

There had been a rawness to the man. Sasha had a quick wit and a discerning intellect. He didn't shy away from any subject. He'd been direct and to the point. And fuck him, but Viktor had liked the guy.

Logic dictated that he should be afraid of him. Sasha Loblaw was a killer. Yet, Viktor had been more intrigued and turned on than afraid for his safety.

Cautiously, he lifted his head from the pillow and turned away from the light. Viktor jerked back—the tempo in his head increased to furious.

His breath caught and his heart rate accelerated.

Sasha. Loblaw. Naked. In bed with him.

Viktor propped up on his elbows and put his head in his hands to think through the crashing noise.

Last night, when he'd left the bar, he'd felt off. They'd sat down on the bench in the lobby. Sasha had led him to sit. That was the last thing he remembered.

Could this be the work of the Cigarette Man?

Viktor hadn't told him he was going to make contact. And he'd said nothing about drugs. That just didn't feel right.

Viktor was supposed to warn the man before he propositioned Sasha.

Had he been played by Sasha Loblaw? But what did Sasha expect to get out of this? Sasha had much more to lose if he was discovered in a compromising position in a hotel room with a man. That pounding in his skull took on a more ominous meaning.

Viktor had been drugged. He thought back to last night and while, yes, they had downed a bunch of drinks, it shouldn't have been enough to incapacitate him. Thanks to his parents and his heritage, he had the constitution of an ox and the classic alcohol tolerance of his Cossack ancestors.

His mouth was dry and his throat felt as if his Hunter Pro knife had scraped him raw.

He assessed his body in other ways, but he seemed to be fine. He had no idea what Sasha had given him, but hopefully the effects would be temporary.

He pushed up to sitting and fought the nausea swirling in his stomach. His gaze tracked around the room, wondering if there were cameras on him right now.

Gingerly, he turned around propped the pillows against the headboard and leaned back, crossing his arms over his chest. Then he watched Sasha, waiting for him to wake up so they could have this out.

While he waited, he absorbed the scents in the room and

the sounds farther afield. The scent of lemon must be in their cleaning products. He inhaled deeply and try as he might, he detected no evidence of sex. Thank God. If he had sex with Sasha, he wanted to remember it.

The remote sound of a vacuum cleaner was faint.

It was a standard high-end room with a king-sized bed and an Asian influence to the décor. A couple of end tables. Their clothes strewn over the gray carpeting and draped over the chair next to the desk. Cell phones rested on top of the desk opposite the bed.

Nothing much penetrated the late morning cocoon of silence except the soft exhale of Sasha Loblaw's breath.

Viktor waited, trying to remember more about last night. He'd been paying close attention to Sasha. No way had the man put anything in his drink. He would have seen him. He must have had help lacing his cosmo. Viktor didn't do drugs. As a medic, he'd seen the ravages that illegal substances wrought on the human body. He didn't typically drink too much either. Remnants of his father's alcohol abuse lingered, and he was careful to respect that dangerous temptation.

As he waited, he studied the sexy Russian spy.

His presence wasn't diminished by the fact that he was asleep. Even in slumber he exuded a raw, dominating presence. His body was finely honed and capable of great violence. But perhaps also capable of incredible sensual attention.

Viktor's erection didn't care that the man was off limits, that Sasha had clearly incapacitated him. He rose like a heat seeking-missile searching for a target. When he'd pictured them in bed together, it certainly hadn't been like this.

Dammit.

* * *

*S*asha woke in an instant, but he didn't move.

There was someone in bed with him.

His brain fogged. He took in the smells. A spicy scent that smelled somewhat familiar dominated everything else, but he couldn't quite place the origin. Fainter smells—a cleaner with a lemon scent, a hint of bleach—underlay that lingering spicy aroma.

The sheets were silky and smooth beneath his body. He was naked. He never slept naked. You couldn't be ready to exfiltrate in an instant if you didn't have clothes on.

Something was very wrong. He tested the area around him with his senses—everything but sight. The unknown subject was to his right. The air to his left felt empty. However, he was clearly off his game since he couldn't remember a damn thing.

Getting out of bed and protecting himself was his number one priority, but his legs were tangled in the sheets, his left foot outside the bunched up material and hanging slightly off the bed. Infinitesimally slowly, he slid his palm underneath his pillow, just in case he was wrong. But the Makarov pistol he normally slept with was not within reaching distance—as was his standard routine.

Light streamed in from the window. He bunched his muscles, ready to jump out of bed. In a burst of movement, he threw off the sheets, jumped out of the bed, and crouched into a fighting stance, facing the threat that had been next to him.

Viktor Kuznets sat propped up in the bed arms over his very nicely muscled chest, eyes narrowed in disgust.

"What the hell did you do to me?" Sasha didn't let down his guard but quickly took in his surroundings, looking for other combatants.

"Nice try, comrade." Viktor skimmed his gaze over Sasha's body.

Sasha's cock, which had been interested in Viktor yesterday, ignored the fact that the man was his enemy, and arrowed toward Viktor.

On his chest was an intricate tattoo of angel wings spread across his pectorals.

"I've got to admit, I didn't expect you to drug me." Viktor's accusation jerked his attention away from the man's beautiful chest.

Viktor kept his gaze on him, and Sasha got lost in those green eyes for a moment. Wait, no. That was crazy. He couldn't afford to be attracted to Viktor. For so, so many reasons.

But he was so caught up in his feelings that it took a second for Viktor's words to register. "I didn't drug you. *You* drugged *me.*"

"Ha." Viktor shook his head. "I don't think so."

"So…what is this? Kompromat?" Sasha didn't let down his guard. "Better men than you have tried." And failed. And most of them ended up dead.

"Listen, dude," Viktor snarled. "You've got a hell of a lot more to lose in this situation than I do. And to think I was worried about you."

There was something in there that Sasha needed to examine later, but right now his priority was to get to the bottom of this situation. "I'm assuming you have pictures, photos that you think you can use for blackmail."

For an infinitesimal second, something uncomfortable flashed across Viktor's face. "I don't remember a damn thing. So I seriously doubt that I have pictures of you. Now tell me why you drugged me and let's get on with this. Cut the shit."

Sasha could appreciate that Viktor didn't beat around the bush.

"Did you use a condom?" Sasha had no sexually

transmitted infections, but that was because he was very, very careful.

"Shit." Viktor patted the covers as if looking for wrappers. "I am fine, are you?"

No way was Sasha answering that. He was extremely discreet.

"If you are going to blackmail me, or try, can you get on with it?" Viktor lifted the covers, looked under the sheets and then huffed in disgust. "I've got a hell of a headache."

Maybe Sasha's brain was still under the effects of the drugs, but he couldn't figure out why Viktor hadn't started in on his blackmail demands. Sasha wanted to glance around the hotel room looking for his clothes, but he kept his attention firmly on Viktor. "What did you do with my clothes?"

He still hadn't relaxed his guard, waiting for some sort of attack.

Viktor ignored him and slid out of bed. Sasha swallowed. The man was gorgeous.

Viktor glanced at Sasha, his gaze dipping to Sasha's cock— which still had not gotten the message that Viktor was the enemy, and stood semi-erect, ready to go with a minimum of provocation.

"You realize any pictures you have of me and you in bed together will implicate you as well?" Viktor casually strode across the room, collecting clothing from the floor as he went. He ignored Sasha, separating the collection of pants and shirts and underwear into two piles.

Doubt crept in. If Viktor was playing him, the man was a good actor. "You really did not have anything to do with this?"

Viktor snorted. "You think?"

Sasha rubbed his head. "Wait a minute, wait a minute." The pounding in his head had only gotten worse. Because why would someone put the two of them in a hotel room together?

"I didn't do this," Sasha said.

"Right." The sarcasm was clear.

Something was very, very wrong. Sasha hadn't done this. And he was beginning to think that possibly Viktor had not either.

Sasha's brain kicked into gear as he watched Viktor feel around the frame of the mirror over the small desk across from the bed. "You expect me to believe that you didn't drug me, strip my clothes off, and get into bed with me."

Sasha's brain stuttered at the word *strip*.

"Right back at you." So someone had wanted them in this room together, naked. "Does someone have a grudge against you?" Sasha asked Viktor, mentally cursing because the man was right. Even if this hadn't been planned, and Sasha had only been a convenient patsy, it would still be worse for him than it would be for Viktor.

If someone had pictures of them together.

"Again, this situation won't affect me. You're the one who has more to lose." Viktor pulled his jeans on over his bare ass. His very fine, muscular, bare ass.

Gav-no, Sasha clearly wasn't thinking straight since he was distracted by the man's butt.

"I need a shower." If the room was bugged, turning on the water was the only way they could talk. It was a gamble, but he had to try. "You want to join me?"

* * *

*W*hat? Viktor jerked to a halt in the process of pulling on his shirt so he could get the hell out.

His mouth was dry, and it wasn't all from the drugs. Sasha hid an incredible body beneath those loose-fitting suits. He wasn't very big, and the suits had been too large for his frame.

That's why it had been difficult to see that underneath his clothing, his body was gorgeous.

For a moment, Viktor's brain blanked. What would it be like to take a shower with him, to press him up against the tiled wall and kiss him until they were both breathless? Water pouring over their bodies as they lost themselves in each other.

As if he had a conduit to Viktor's brain, Sasha's cock rose.

But Viktor didn't think he was truly inviting him into the shower for sex. *Unfortunately.*

"After you."

Sasha sauntered into the bathroom, completely unconcerned with his nudity. He leaned over the tub and turned on the shower. Viktor followed him into the bathroom and closed the door quietly.

As if they had worked together for years, they checked the room for hidden recording devices. After a thorough vetting of the light fixtures, the mirror, even the hardware that held the toilet paper and towel racks, and the fan system, they nodded at each other.

No audio or video recording devices were found.

Sasha leaned closer to him and for a moment, his scent enveloped Viktor in a cloud. Lust clawed at his insides, and he wanted to forget that something was rotten about this set up and kiss the man senseless.

"I didn't drug you." Sasha's breath shivered over his neck and ear.

He replied quietly, "I didn't drug you either."

"Someone wanted us in this room together." Sasha tested the water, as if he were going to get in the shower.

"Any ideas who that might be?" Viktor couldn't help but think of the nameless Cigarette Man in Jill's office. Could he have engineered drugging them both and putting them in the room together? The man had never said a word about incapacitating Viktor on his mission and Viktor hadn't told him he was going to recon on Sasha. "What's the last thing you remember?"

"We walked out of the bar and into the hotel lobby."

Viktor wracked his brain, but that was his last memory as well. He'd felt a little fuzzy but put it down to his lack of sleep over the last two weeks. He needed to talk to Jill. He needed to find out exactly who that man was. But just in case this was a setup by Sasha, Viktor wasn't going to confess that he'd been blackmailed into compromising Sasha.

"We sat on the bench." Women. The vague sense of a soft hand against his face and red lips flashed through his brain. "Women?"

"Not that I recall."

So maybe that was some other memory?

"Who would gain from pictures of you?" Sasha interrupted as Viktor tried to pull that image of a woman from his foggy brain. "Of us?"

"I have no idea."

Sasha looked at him steadily. As if he could see into his soul and he knew that Viktor was lying. "You need to go."

Viktor didn't know why, but he knew that he had disappointed Sasha. And that ate at him. Although why he should care about a man he just met and what he thought of Viktor, he couldn't comprehend.

"I can't trust you." Viktor hated to admit it, but Sasha needed to know where he stood.

Sasha barked out a laugh. "That's not news."

Viktor skimmed his gaze over Sasha's naked body, regret filling him. "I'll be in touch." Because sure as hell whoever did this had more planned for them both.

Chapter 6

*V*iktor left the bathroom before he did something completely ill-advised and inappropriate. He grabbed the rest of his stuff from the chair in the corner.

He always carried two weapons on him. Last night, he'd brought a tactical telescoping baton and his Hunter Pro, lock blade, five-and-a-half-inch knife. The knife was with his wallet, but the baton was missing. It was possible he'd lost it when they'd been sitting on the bench. But he certainly didn't like the implication. At least his knife was still with his things.

He ruthlessly went through Sasha's pockets looking for any incriminating evidence. But the man's cell was a cheap burner. He had a cool grand in cash and a set of car keys. A nondescript Ford Taurus would be Viktor's guess. Sasha carried nothing identifiable on him. Even his clothes were custom made, but without labels.

Viktor opened his own wallet and checked to see if all his cash was there and his identification. He hadn't been trying to hide anything.

The sound of the shower beat on his consciousness, and he tried to erase from his brain the vision of Sasha Loblaw naked.

Jesus, the man was built. His clothes hid a cut physique; the muscles in his abdomen arrowed like a giant sign pointing to his most impressive cock. Viktor's mouth watered at the memory. As he adjusted the collar of his shirt, in the mirror he noticed a red stain on the placket. Frowning, he leaned in to get a closer look.

Was that...lipstick? Viktor raised one eyebrow and studied the smear for another moment. Well, that was an interesting development. He strode over to the television and turned it on, searching the hotel's on screen menu for a copy of the bill, but it was blank.

Viktor tucked his wallet and phone into his jeans pocket and headed to the front desk. Maybe he could get some intelligence from them.

"Hello, I'd like to check out of Room 213."

"Certainly, sir." The attractive Black woman behind the desk smiled at him. "Would you like a copy of your bill?"

"Yes, please." Perhaps he could get some intelligence from who paid the bill for this hotel room.

"Here you go, Mr. Smith." The smiling young woman handed him a single sheet of paper with the hotel logo and a final total of close to five hundred dollars. Whoever did this should have realized that Viktor couldn't afford that on his salary. He made good money at ALIAS, but five hundred a night was way out of his reach.

Mr. Smith? They couldn't have gotten more creative?

Viktor scanned the bill, looked at the address listed for Mr. Smith as 2301 I Street Northwest. If he wasn't mistaken, that was the address of the Foggy Bottom Metro station.

Most of the credit card number on file was blocked out, but maybe he'd be able to discover the rest with some online digging. He glanced around the fancy lobby and wondered if he could find someone with the clout to access the security cameras.

"I'm all set. Thanks."

He ducked around the corner just to make sure he hadn't somehow dropped the baton on the floor by the bench, but it was clear.

Viktor cast one last regretful glance at the elevators and then headed home. He needed to assess what to do next. First go into the office and talk to Jill. Maybe see if Kita could pull anything from a computer search on the bill. He headed for the garage attached to the hotel.

His head throbbed in time with his thoughts.

Random thoughts kept pinging around in his brain. The seed of an idea was just out of reach, but he couldn't quite pull it to the forefront of his mind. If he could just figure out why someone had drugged them, maybe the seed would take root and the idea would blossom into something actionable.

Viktor got into his six-year-old Chevy Silverado and sent a prayer of thanks for the fact that he hadn't driven while seriously impaired.

Viktor placed both his hands on the steering wheel at the ten and two positions and rested his head against the hard plastic. He breathed in and then out slowing his heart rate and trying not to freak out about all the potential negative consequences of last night.

He pulled out his phone to text Jillian, but something about his lock screen stopped him midway through his logon. It was a picture that he knew he hadn't taken.

He was wearing the clothes from last night. His arm hooked around Sasha's neck, they were both smiling for the camera as if they hadn't a care in the world, and two scantily clad, buxom young women hung on their shoulders, bookending the men between them. If Viktor wasn't mistaken, the lipstick on his shirt had come from the woman draped all over him. The women had their heads turned so that they were mostly in profile, staring at the men as if they wanted to jump them.

From the angle it was difficult to tell their race. Their hair mostly hid their features, especially their ears, and their facial structure. They could be white but the picture was slightly overexposed, so that could be a result of the flash rather than their actual skin tone.

Most people would look and see two men with female sex workers, but when Viktor looked at the picture, he saw him and Sasha in a quasi-embrace.

Now that was kind of funny. Whoever set this up didn't realize that he was gay. He thought it was obvious and he didn't hide his sexuality, but clearly someone hadn't done their homework.

When he opened the photos tab, there were two more pictures of all of them but again it was impossible to see the women's faces. Both he and Sasha were naked from the waist up with the equally naked women draped over them. The photos were raunchy, but unlikely to cause trouble for Sasha or Viktor.

They were definitely not the kind of photographs that the Cigarette Man had wanted. Something in Viktor eased. He hadn't lied to Sasha.

He sighed and put the phone away. He would head straight to Adams-Larsen and see if he could figure out the time that these photographs were taken. Then he'd contact Sasha. But a sense of relief washed over him at this moment. There were no compromising photos of just the two of them. Viktor could rest easy that whatever happened last night wouldn't give Sasha a death sentence.

Viktor turned the key in the ignition and the car roared to

life. He wasn't thinking clearly. He should have checked for explosives. But, so far, so good. He put his truck into drive and gave one last longing glance at the hotel. When he'd arrived at the bar last evening, he hadn't foreseen this ending.

But luckily whoever did this—scratch that—*hopefully* whoever did this left clues he could follow like breadcrumbs, and he would get to the bottom of whatever happened last night.

* * *

Sasha stayed in the shower overly long, not wanting to deal with Viktor again. Waking up in bed with Viktor underscored all the ways that he couldn't have the man. It would be the height of irony if it turned out someone got kompromat when he hadn't even done the deed. Whatever happened last night pretty much destroyed any possibility that some time in the nebulous future, Viktor and Sasha would get together.

Sasha didn't trust the man. There'd been something in his gaze—a flicker of guilt?—when he'd asked about someone wanting to set them up that said Viktor knew something about who wanted him compromised. Sasha had to wonder who? And why? Blackmail? Although Viktor seemed genuinely shocked about being drugged.

Was the FSB setting Sasha up?

Or could the United States government be setting him up?

He'd been suspicious of this assignment from the beginning, especially the way the ambassador shoved Viktor at him as a potential lead on the traitor case and the way he insisted that Sasha begin his investigation with Viktor.

Sasha had too many questions and no answers.

When he figured he'd been in the shower long enough, he

shut off the water and quickly used the towel to dry off. But his body and brain were remembering the sight of Viktor sitting up against the sheets, that magnificent angel wing tattoo spread across his thickly muscled chest, and a hard light in his bright green eyes that should not have been a turn on. But it was.

Viktor Kuznets could hold his own with Sasha. He would bet that if they'd had the chance, they would have combusted.

He shrugged off the longing and regret. He tugged on his clothing quickly and paused. He lifted his sweater.

Perfume tickled his nose.

Definitely perfume, not cologne. Besides, he had catalogued everything about Viktor Kuznets in the bar last night and he hadn't been wearing cologne. A subtle scented deodorant perhaps but nothing as effeminate as cologne. This was straight up perfume. He sniffed again and a flash of memory hit him.

A woman, hanging all over him, pressing up against him and running her lips along his neck.

A woman. Interesting.

He searched his pockets, but they held only the cash he carried for emergencies, one thousand US, and his car keys. Everything was anonymous and not labeled. Even his suits had no labels. Nothing that could be identified as his. He shrugged into the oversize button-down and pulled on his suit pants. The slightly too big clothes diminished the threat of his body and frequently led people to underestimate him. They either saw him as a little bit scrawny, or perhaps sometimes sickly. It was a disguise that had served him well for the past twenty odd years. He found himself wishing he had dressed in a showy manner, like a peacock flaunting its feathers so he could have preened in front of Viktor and ignited his desire.

Just thinking about him caused Sasha to chub up.

He searched the room once more, then leaned over the bed looking for any clues to what had happened. On one of the pillows was a smudge of lipstick. Women. The women had been *in bed* with both of them?

Even that wasn't enough to blackmail Sasha. But perhaps whoever had set this up didn't realize that. He wondered what their endgame was and then wondered how long he'd have to wait to find out.

Somehow, he thought that whatever the con, whatever the blackmail plan, it involved both him and Viktor. With that, he realized with a thrill that most likely he would be seeing Viktor Kuznets again.

He couldn't wait.

He needed to file his report regarding last night. The question became did he confess to being drugged, and most likely had incriminating photos taken of him, or did he leave it? He was tempted not to confess, because perhaps this had been set up by his own government. Perhaps this entire situation had been to make Sasha look ineffective and careless, as if he could no longer do his job. Then he could be retired.

Whatever the reason, it didn't pay to lie to his superiors. He had on occasion done so, on purpose, but as far as he knew they had not caught on to him yet.

He was going to have to come up with some valid reason why Viktor was not the agent they were looking for. The urge to check his exit strategy bank account was strong, but he couldn't do anything that raised suspicion.

Sasha glanced around the hotel room once more and wished, not for the first time, that it had just been him and Viktor in this room and that it had ended in quite a different way.

Chapter 7

Viktor trudged into the office. As he did every morning, he placed his hand on the biometric scanner and recited the Pledge of Allegiance.

He hadn't been born in this country and he was thankful every day for the opportunities that Jillian and Marsh had given him. He had vague memories of his home in Russia. But what he remembered most was being cold and afraid.

That hadn't really changed when they had come to America. In New York, his family had been cold, afraid, and hungry. It had not been the land of opportunity his father had expected, and the man had been bitterly unhappy. That bitterness had permeated everything about Viktor's childhood. His parents embraced American culture and finally found their purpose. But it had been a long, hard road. His father had taken to drinking cheap alcohol when he was frustrated, taking out his disappointment and his rage on Viktor and his mother.

That disappointment had only grown when his father began to realize that Viktor did not want women. The more his father had pushed, the more Viktor had resisted.

ALIAS was more than a job to him. They were his family. And he let them down once. He had more shame over that mistake than he did over coming out of his sexuality with his parents.

His parents were old-school Russia, and they refused to acknowledge that homosexuality was real. After getting out of the US Army, when he refused to hide his true nature any longer, they had disowned him.

Their lack of acceptance had gutted him which was why he craved the acceptance of his colleagues. He smiled hello at Kita and Dwayne and went to grab a cup of tea from the sideboard in the conference room.

He had taken one sip of the hot liquid when Marsh paged him.

"I need you to follow this woman." Marsh gave a quick rundown of Ayesha Brown. Young, Black, artist, and possibly in trouble.

Viktor nodded, determined to do the best job he possibly could. He wasn't going to let down his friends again.

He popped his head into Jillian's office, but she was on the phone. She waved him in. He approached silently and sat in the chair across from her desk while he waited for her to be done.

She finally hung up, her eyes sparkling. "What can I do for you?"

"I made contact." His stomach roiled and he didn't want to admit that he woken up in bed with their target, but he wasn't going to keep things from Jillian.

"How did it go?"

Viktor rubbed his face with his hands and took a deep breath. "I wound up in bed with him."

"What?" Jillian looked sick. "I told you that you didn't have to sleep with him."

"I don't think I did."

She blinked. "You don't *think*?"

"I believe I was drugged."

She surged out of her chair. "Are you okay?"

Viktor's heart warmed. "I seem to be fine."

"That wasn't discussed as a possible scenario."

Viktor said, "I know. But I don't know if it was the Cigarette Man."

Jill snorted. "Cigarette Man?"

"He carried the slight scent of tobacco." Viktor shrugged with his hands up. "And since I don't know his name…"

"The less you know about him the better. That way you have plausible deniability."

She was looking out for him.

"So you think Loblaw drugged you." Jill continued. "What was his endgame? Do you think he suspected you of targeting him?"

He thought about the shock on Sasha's face, and the anger he had directed at Viktor. "I don't think he did it."

"Then who did?"

Viktor had been going over the night endlessly, trying to figure out when someone could have slipped something in his drink. The answer he came up with was that only the bartender had been near his drink. "I think it was the bartender. But obviously he was just a pawn."

"Name?" Jillian's fingers were poised on her laptop.

"I don't know. Mack somebody." Viktor shook his head. "I'm going to go back later today and question him."

"Okay."

"Can you get in touch with Cigarette Man? See if I have inadvertently satisfied the terms of our agreement." Because he certainly hadn't done so on purpose.

"But I don't like that you were drugged. That was not in the parameters of what he asked."

Viktor wasn't thrilled about it either. "I hadn't told him I was going to the bar last night."

"I'll see what I can find out."Jill tapped a finger on her desk, her eyes far away.

His stomach still hadn't recovered, the acid sloshing around like waves on the Potomac. "I woke up naked in bed with him. There may be pictures I am unaware of. I have some pictures on my phone of the four of us."

"Back up. Four? And naked?"

"Partially undressed. But we are with women."

Maybe this was it. Their obligation to the mystery man was over and ALIAS would be safe. They could try to return to normal. But the women didn't make sense.

"Have Kita run facial recognition on the women," Jill said.

"We aren't just going to assume this is what he wanted and go about our business."

"Hell no."

His shoulders relaxed. The whole situation wasn't sitting well with him. The man had indicated that he wanted kompromat on Sasha, but an orgy wouldn't matter to anyone. "What are the odds that someone else drugged us?" It had to be the Cigarette Man. Right?

"We'll figure it out." Jill told him, and his worry eased some more. "I have your back."

"Can I share anything else with Kita?" Cigarette Man hadn't indicated that they had to keep his little side mission secret. If Viktor thought about their brief meeting, the man had been spare with details.

Jill said, "I know you won't like this, but share as little as possible. You'll need to tell her about the drugs and the women. Otherwise, the less she knows, the better."

Jill was right. He didn't like it.

"What's the goal here?" Jill tapped her pen on the fancy leather-trimmed blotter on her desktop. "Pictures with women won't hurt Loblaw."

"I don't know." Maybe it was the aftereffects of whatever drug he'd been given, but he still couldn't seem to put together any credible reason, any blackmail strategy, to explain why someone would drug him and Sasha and put them in bed together *with women.*

"You're the medic. Can you pull your blood and see if anything strange comes up in the sample?"

A clear indication he wasn't thinking well. He should have thought of that. "Ten four."

His stomach roiled at the thought of blood, but he pushed it aside. He'd like to know what he'd been given. Identifying the drug could provide clues to who had been behind their drugging.

"Are you okay?"

Viktor's heart warmed. Jillian looked out for them all. So did Marsh. "I will be."

But he wondered…would he? And when?

* * *

*A*fter taking a blood sample and prepping it to drop off at the lab, Viktor headed to Kita's office.

After the standard pleasantries, she said, "What's up?"

He pulled out his phone, clicked on the pictures of the women. "I'm sending you a couple of pictures. Can you run facial recognition on these women and see if you get any hits?"

He emailed the pictures to Kita's ALIAS address. She clicked on the pictures. "Umm, what the what?"

He flushed.

"What's happening here?" Kita studied the pictures. "Your pupils are blown. And you've got lipstick on your shirt."

"It's complicated."

"You switching teams?" she teased.

He didn't want to admit that he'd lost time, that he'd been bamboozled again. He was still recovering from his mistake of trusting Malachi Walsh. But he wasn't in the habit of keeping secrets. There were already too many. "I was drugged."

"By him?"

Viktor tried to keep his face impassive, but Kita knew him well enough to know that he was a terrible liar. Everyone in the office knew he couldn't lie worth shit.

"I'm not sure." Viktor shrugged. "The other man is possibly another victim."

"That guy looks like no one's victim."

True. He'd hate to be the person who drugged them when Sasha Loblaw caught up with him or her.

She studied the photo some more. "You went to a hotel room with strangers?"

He couldn't bear for her to be disappointed in him. "It was for a case."

Kita tilted her head. "Which one?"

"You're better off not knowing." Jill hadn't expressly forbidden him, but he didn't want to put Kita in jeopardy. The last thing he wanted was to pull Kita into this mess. "I just need to see if I can track down these women."

Confirm who hired them. Ask them about their mission objective. Find out exactly what happened and who had taken the pictures. Were they selfies or had someone else been in that room with them?

"You don't want any intelligence on the guy." It wasn't a question, but she looked slightly confused.

"Uh, no."

"I'll run their partials through a database. But it could take a while." She studied the women. "Clothes are expensive. Their makeup is flawless. The wigs—"

"Wigs?"

"Sure." She pointed to the hairline on the one with the choppy layers. "If you look closely, you can see a bit of black hair beneath the caramel-colored layers."

Viktor peered closer. Huh. She was right.

She continued. "Which would make sense. Based on her cheekbones and the line of her jaw, she might be part Asian. The angle of the picture makes it hard to identify which nationality. Maybe Korean. Maybe Chinese. Even Vietnamese is a possibility. But speculating isn't optimal."

Viktor's brain was starting to fire smoothly again, like a well-oiled trigger. "They are high-end sex workers."

Kita grimaced. "It's a booming business in this town."

Viktor nodded. She wasn't wrong.

"Judging by their appearance and skin and muscle tone, they take really good care of their bodies. I don't see any needle tracks or signs of drug use. They might be voluntarily selling their bodies."

He heard something in her voice. "That upsets you?"

"If it's their free will, I have no right to object."

"But…"

"There are all sorts of ways to coerce people." Kita was clearly conflicted.

Viktor speculated. "If they aren't trafficked or drug addicted, they may be easier to track down." A madam or escort service would likely use an online booking app with a website so the clients could choose their preference. But they could also potentially pay in less easily identified and tracked currency, like Bitcoin.

"Don't count on answers." Kita's fingers clacked over the

keyboard as she worked her hacking magic. "They have to keep their employers' and clients' secrets or they won't last long in DC."

"True. But I still might be able to get something out of them if we can track them down and I can talk to them."

Kita nodded.

"Can you make sure that our IP is blocked and shielded?" No need to let the Cigarette Man know they were following up if he was the one who engineered this.

"Can you field strip a Beretta 92 in mere seconds?"

Viktor should know better than to question his friend. She was a professional and very good at her job. "Acknowledged."

Kita's brow crinkled. "I thought we were past the trust thing."

"I apologize." He was still not quite recovered. And he needed to get his blood sample to a lab.

"Did they steal anything?"

"No." At least not that he was aware of. "Um, although maybe I should check my bank account."

"If they didn't rob you, what was their mission objective?"

Put money in his bank account? Make it look like he had received money in exchange for the pictures.

He wouldn't put it past the Cigarette Man to put safeguards in place to secure Viktor's cooperation—if he was the one who did this. "That's a very good question."

Kita studied the pictures again. "He's hot."

Yes. Yes, he was. Nuclear hot. "Yes."

"Could he have had something to do with whatever is going on that you and Jill aren't talking about?"

"Possibly." Viktor wasn't about to rule out Sasha. But he had seemed very convincing when he'd accused Viktor of drugging him. However, he was a known FSB agent with many years of experience. He would be an expert at lying and covering his tracks.

His background should have made him scary and intimidating. But all Viktor could focus on was the incredible physical attraction he'd felt. Was it hot in here?

"What happened?"

"We struck up a conversation at the bar and this morning we woke up in bed together." He began to sweat remembering the smooth expanse of Sasha's skin and the power hidden beneath those loose suits.

"All four of you?"

"The women were gone."

"So just you and the hottie?"

"Yes. And a phone with those pictures." Viktor sighed.

Kita shifted her gaze from the pictures to Viktor. "You're attracted to him."

"Unimportant." Viktor would never let himself be swayed by a pretty—or in this case, arresting and compelling—face. "I would never betray ALIAS."

"I know that." She nudged him with her shoulder. "You have to forgive yourself."

Impossible. He wanted so badly to belong somewhere, to someone. How could he have jeopardized that because of a hot body and loneliness?

"It was one mistake." She squeezed his bicep. "That anyone could make." He didn't understand how she could be so forgiving. He could have seriously jeopardized everyone at ALIAS.

He slashed his hand. "But anyone didn't make it. I did."

"Hooking up with someone in a bar isn't against the rules." Kita shot back.

Now that was funny. "Since when do you care about rules?" Kita lived to break them.

She laughed. "Apparently Alex is growing on me."

She had met her boyfriend on an op a few months ago when they had worked together to guard a federal judge and fallen in love. These days she walked around smiling. She was still a badass. Just a badass with a smile on her face.

"Go scare up Jake and spar. Or beat up the bag…just stop beating up yourself." She waved him out of her office. "I'll call you when I have a hit on the women."

* * *

Sasha left the hotel cautiously, doing standard checks for bugs, surveillance, and anyone who might be paying too much attention to his movements. But nothing, and no one, stood out. He took an extended surveillance detection route back to his apartment by rote action.

Half his brain was focused on what Viktor Kuznets might want from him and what the man had hoped to accomplish with last night's stunt, and the other half on the memory of Viktor's tattooed chest and rippled abs.

He turned over the entire night in his mind, mentally retracing every step from the beginning of the evening to this morning. Sasha had been paying close attention to their surroundings and the other patrons in the bar while he and Viktor were bantering. There was no way the man had put anything in his drink.

The drug had hit him while he'd been leaving. Which meant the bartender was likely the culprit. Hopefully the server would be a weak link.

Sasha pulled up his records search program, proprietary software developed by the FSB, on his laptop to locate the man who he believed drugged him and Viktor.

He had decided to hold off on filing his report about last

night's disaster until he gathered more intelligence. After all, he'd questioned Viktor regarding the shooting death of Sergei Polzin as requested. He'd asked the man to share if he discovered any more intelligence surrounding the former Russian. He needed to write that up. The request from his boss seemed flimsy at best. Sasha had done his own research and there had been chatter about Polzin and the shooting. It just seemed too coincidental to him.

He still wasn't convinced that the Russian government wasn't trying to discredit or decommission him. He wanted more information about the entire situation before he confessed to his superiors regarding the loss of his memory and faculties.

There was absolutely no way he'd revealed any state secrets. He'd been trained by the best interrogators in the world to resist all forms of persuasion. He'd have never been allowed in the field if he'd exhibited any weakness for drugs or torture. And he would never have lasted in his job if he were weak or ineffective.

Initially his service had been conscripted without his consent, but he was just ornery enough that he refused to do a bad job. He'd excelled at every task they had given him. He'd moved up the chain of command and become an active participant in some horrible things.

His loyalty to Russia, to Putin, to the FSB, had been rewarded. Doled out in small increments. He had power, and some money, enough to enjoy the finer things in life, but little agency. Until recently the government had held the threat of harm to his mother over him—as long as he had done what they asked, he had status and his mother was safe.

He flexed his hands, remembering the torture he'd endured as part of his training.

He doubted seriously that the flirty bartender had had the same training.

He shut down his laptop and stored the encrypted equipment in a safe located in a hidden compartment beneath the floorboards under his bed.

The bartender's name was Manuel (Mack) Garcia. Armed with his home address, Sasha decided to do some surveillance on the most likely candidate who had drugged him...and Viktor.

That assumed that Viktor had been telling the truth and he hadn't had anything to do with their incapacitation. If not, who was intended the target? Sasha or Viktor? Or...both?

Sasha took the Metro, switching trains, and doubling back several times before exiting at a station several blocks from the bartender's apartment.

According to the hotel records he had hacked, the bartender had been on duty until closing at two a.m. After closing, he would have taken inventory and cleaned up the bar before going home. So he likely wouldn't have gone to bed until after four a.m. He lived in a working-class section of Virginia with four other roommates in a two-bedroom, one-bathroom apartment.

It was only nine in the morning, so Mack was probably still asleep. Two roommates worked food service/hospitality jobs and kept late hours. The other three worked nine-to-five jobs in the district and should already be gone. From the coffee shop kitty corner to the apartment building, Sasha watched the entrance and exits of the building.

He wore jeans and a nondescript sweatshirt with a Washington Nationals cap covering his hair and shielding his eyes. He had added a little padding to his cheeks and a prosthetic belly over his waist.

He ordered a frou-frou coffee and read the *Washington Post* in paper form while surreptitiously studying both the apartment building and the inhabitants of the coffee shop.

The clientele was a mix of stay-at-home parents with kids in strollers and work-from-home employees with headsets, either constantly on their phone or pounding on their laptops.

The Metrobus doors hissed open and let out several passengers. Several people walked the opposite way. Only one man, wearing dirty coveralls and a ratty old ball cap with an indistinguishable logo, carrying a tool kit, headed straight to the building, walking slowly as if he'd was tired after working a full shift.

Tenants exited the building and caught the bus.

After an hour of surveillance, Sasha stood. Time to get up close and personal with the bartender. He'd accessed the man's bank accounts and yesterday Mack had received a deposit of five thousand dollars, which was more than suspicious since most of his money came in cash tips that were untraceable and not typically reported to the American government.

It was no wonder the man had potentially taken some minimum risk spy work for a decent payoff. He lived paycheck to paycheck, got most of his meals as freebies from work, and spent his off nights at a local gay bar trolling for a sugar daddy. He tended to date older, powerful men.

Based on the deposits in his checking account, cash infusions in five grand pops over the past month, either he had found one or he had started doing "favors" for several people.

As a bartender, he was in a unique position to overhear sensitive information. Although Sasha always exchanged classified intelligence in private, many in Washington were not as discreet. Get a few drinks in an underpaid, overworked congressional aide and plenty could be learned. Or listen to drunk congressmen bragging at taxpayer-funded wine-and-dines about their classified intelligence access.

He pulled on his gloves, folded up the newspaper, and tucked it under his arm. He strolled leisurely down the street away from the bartender's apartment building and dropped the paper in the wastebasket on the sidewalk.

When he reached the next block, he turned right and then right again to double back toward the bartender's apartment building one block over. After evaluating the accessibility of entering the building from the rear, he headed into the parking lot of the building directly behind the bartender's. He maneuvered through a small break in the hedge between the two buildings. Thankfully, no chain link fence hid beneath the wild brambles that separated the parking lots.

He picked the lock on the rear door of the apartment building casually as if he were jiggling his key in the lock. Within seconds he slipped inside the building and headed for the second floor. After moving quietly along the hallway, he paused at the bartender's apartment and considered his options.

Deciding on the direct approach, he knocked sharply on the apartment door.

Sasha waited impatiently. But no one answered.

He rapped on the door again and waited.

No one answered. He heard no rustling from inside the apartment. The bartender could have picked up a lover for the night and wasn't home yet, but the only way to find out was to check.

Sasha pulled out his lockpicks and quickly jimmied the apartment lock.

He slipped into the apartment quietly and shut the door with a soft snick. The curtains were open in the living room and sunlight poured into the dirty apartment. Clothes and shoes were strewn about the floor and dumped on the furniture. An empty pizza box on the coffee table sat open and discarded. The kitchen was equally as messy, with the dishes piled in the sink, food still on the plates and open beer cans on the counter. Sasha shook his head at the disgusting condition of the apartment and headed toward the bedrooms.

He opened the first bedroom door to more of the same mess. Unmade beds, one twin and the other double were shoved up against the walls with barely room to maneuver between them.

The second bedroom door was closed. It was possible that one of the other roommates was here. Sasha quietly turned the knob and eased open the bedroom door.

The smell hit him first. The coppery scent of blood and the foul smell of recently emptied bowels permeated the small, stifling room. The bartender lay in a twin bed with a rubber tie off wrapped around his bicep and a syringe sticking out of his arm.

Sasha checked for a pulse, but the man was dead. His skin was still warm to the touch.

Fuck.

The overdose was a little too convenient to be accidental. Someone had obviously killed the man after he had done what they'd asked. Someone didn't want Sasha to know why or who had drugged him. *Piz dets.* This just got more complicated.

Based on Mack Garcia's body temperature, the assassin hadn't left long ago.

He thought back to the past hour. Most of the people had been leaving the building. No one stood out. Except the man who'd gotten off the bus in the coveralls. Fuck. Sasha ran through his memory banks, replaying the man's movements, trying to get any kind of imprint of the fellow's face. But he'd kept his back mostly to Sasha. Now that he thought about it, the man had been carrying the toolbox which could have held the paraphernalia needed to shoot Mack up.

The assassin could have been in the building before Sasha arrived at the coffee shop, but the first rule was to get in and get out. You didn't linger. That was how people got caught.

Sasha was too late and any link to who had hired Mack Garcia was likely gone.

He quickly and efficiently searched the apartment, looking for any clues as to who might have hired the bartender. And who might have killed him.

He didn't have it in him to feel sorry for the man.

Blyad.

Viktor was telling the truth. Unless he had hired the bartender and then killed him to keep it quiet. For all his bravado, Viktor Kuznets was not a cold-blooded killer. Sasha knew he had likely killed before. But his job in the Army had been as a medic. He saved people. He didn't hurt them.

Now Sasha wondered, who was the target?

It didn't make sense that his bosses set him up. They were not the subtle sort. If they'd wanted Sasha dead, he'd be on his way to dead. While he had no illusions that he was immortal, he should be able to elude his comrades, at least for awhile. After all, he'd trained most of the people who operated in the US.

So who was behind their drugging? And what did they want?

iktor let himself into his apartment. It had been a shit day. He couldn't believe that Ayesha Brown had tagged him. He was supposed to be working on restoring his credibility, not making it worse.

In stranger news, Marsh seemed a tad bit obsessed with the wily Ms. Brown. He had been impressed with Brown's ability to evade surveillance.

Sure, his boss, Marsh, had told him not to worry about it… but still Viktor's slip up was another demerit in his file.

He would admit that his mind hadn't been completely on the job.

His brain kept flashing back to this morning in the hotel room with Sasha. That moment when Sasha had stood in front of him, naked and unashamed, Viktor had been so damn tempted.

Even with the belief that Sasha had drugged him, his body would have overruled the giant, neon warning in his brain saying that having sex with the FSB operative was a very bad idea. If Sasha had made any move, Viktor would have made the very bad decision in a heartbeat. A feeling of regret came over him when he thought about not getting the chance to know Sasha better.

While they had been at the bar, exchanging playful banter, Viktor felt as if they had connected on a subliminal level. Last night, he knew they'd never be able to pursue their attraction and he'd squashed his regret. Waking up next to Sasha this morning hadn't improved those odds.

That sense of loss, of missing out on something extraordinary, had plagued him all day.

He needed to get over it and get on with his life.

He was still waiting for contact from the Cigarette Man. Viktor had assumed he would be given a heads-up before the guy planned to get pictures. Viktor's goal last night was reconnaissance only.

If Cigarette Man had followed him and drugged him, then Viktor had fulfilled his part of the bargain and Adams-Larsen should get some relief.

No word from Kita on the women. And no word from the lab on what drug he'd been given, if it was even possible to identify.

As soon as he entered his apartment, he realized that his inattention could cost him—again. He reached for a weapon, but it was too late.

The thick arm around his chest and the nick of a blade at his neck stopped him cold. He reassessed the situation and settled into a calm, fighting mindset. He couldn't reach the knife in the holster on his ankle, but he had a stash of weapons around his apartment. He just needed to maneuver the man behind him without telegraphing that Viktor was subtly moving him toward any of the hidden weapons.

"Don't bother." The man nudged Viktor away from the

sofa. In the dim light he saw a pile of weapons on the glass-topped coffee table, and he realized that his intruder had found his stash.

Every single one.

"We're going to have a talk."

A subtle scent teased his senses. Viktor stopped and held still.He knew that scent. His body softened without permission even though he knew he should stay on guard.

"Sasha?"

Sasha Loblaw let Viktor go and pushed him gently toward the ladderback chair in the center of the room. "Sit."

Viktor hesitated. In a fight, physically they'd be evenly matched. Although in sheer underhanded tactics and meanness, Sasha would win. The man was rumored to be one of the best assassins the Russians had. Besides, he wanted to know exactly why Sasha was here. Fighting with him wouldn't accomplish that.

That didn't mean he liked being at Sasha's mercy. He sat reluctantly.

Viktor was trying to get a handle on why Sasha Loblaw was in his apartment. "I didn't drug you."

"I figured that out." Sasha zip-tied his arms behind his back and then restrained his ankles against the chair legs.

"This isn't necessary." Viktor could break the ties easily. He suspected that Sasha knew it.

"It'll slow you down if you decide to attack me."

Sasha stood in front of him. Tonight, he wore skinny jeans that showcased his muscular thighs and the bulge in his pants. A loose sweatshirt hid his defined abs, but Viktor's brain had fantastic recall. His cock rose at the memories assaulting him. Sasha standing in front of him completely naked. Every perfect muscle defined and rippled in the low light of that hotel room.

Even now, in a vulnerable position and at the brutal man's mercy, instead of fight reflex, his body responded to the unexpectedly erotic kink of being restrained. That's not what this was and yet he still couldn't help but react to his scent. He raised his gaze to the deadly spy.

Sasha missed nothing, watching Viktor steadily. His brown eyes darkened with lust. Viktor felt a moment of triumph. He wasn't alone in this inconvenient attraction.

Sasha's gaze dropped to Viktor's crotch, where his cock pushed against his zipper. Sasha smirked and raised an eyebrow.

Two could play at that game. Viktor licked his lips and stared at the man's cock again. Was it even bigger? Had his erection grown?

Sasha finally said, "We need to talk."

Viktor remained silent. He had nothing to say that was relevant to this inquisition. Unless he wanted to play some kind of kinky game.

But as Sasha stood in front of him and studied him, Viktor wanted to squirm. "What?"

"I figured out who drugged us."

Viktor straightened in the chair. "Oh?" Viktor wondered if Sasha also had pictures of the women and them in bed on *his* phone.

"The bartender."

Viktor nodded. That had been his assessment as well. He had planned to question the bartender once he had the lab results from his blood. The Cigarette Man had gotten what he wanted, and Viktor's participation was over. Adams-Larsen had been saved from his stupidity, and they were now protected. Hopefully. But he still had questions. Jill had been equally determined to unearth exactly what was going on. Luckily pictures of women wouldn't hurt Sasha.

"Did he tell you why?" Viktor was curious. He didn't imagine that Mack the bartender could withstand Sasha's tactics if he used standard Russian interrogation techniques.

"He's dead."

Viktor straightened in the chair. "You killed him?" Shit. Had he completely misread Sasha's personality? Killing a random lackey—because no way in hell was the bartender a player—was beyond dumb. Murder tended to draw the attention of the authorities and getting noticed should be anathema to what Sasha did. Of course, Viktor had been wrong about people before.

"Of course not." Sasha ran his hand through his dark hair. "He was dead when I got there."

He paced in front of Viktor. Viktor had the uncomfortable realization that Sasha was sharing information with him. That made Viktor feel guilty because he had set him up. Or at least he had had a hand in setting him up.

But why would the Cigarette Man kill the bartender? He flashed back to Jillian's office. The Cigarette Man had been smug, confident that Viktor would fall in line. But he worked for the government.

If Cigarette Man had killed Mack…was Viktor next? Or Jill? Viktor began to work to escape his bindings. This information changed things.

Sasha stopped pacing. "Did you kill him?"

Viktor jerked back. "What? No. Of course not."

"Okay." Sasha rubbed his palm over his clean-shaven jaw.

Sasha seemed to accept Viktor's denial awfully quickly. But since Viktor hadn't had anything to do with Mack's death, he was glad the assassin believed him.

"Any idea who did kill him?" Viktor grasped for any information on the bartender's death that might make sense. Viktor wasn't naïve enough to believe that the US government never killed people. However, they didn't typically kill US citizens on US soil. There were rules that, as far as he knew, the government followed. "How did he die?"

"Overdose."

"Maybe it was an accident."

Sasha raised his eyebrows. "Really?"

"Right." Viktor shook his head. "Too convenient."

"Especially since I'm having difficulty tracing the origin of the five thousand US dollars he received." Sasha rubbed his jaw again. "The money is still in his account—whoever killed him must be decently funded and unconcerned about the cash being traced to them. They didn't take it back."

Viktor agreed with that assessment. Which didn't give him warm fuzzies. Otherwise, why not take the money back? "They?"

Sasha said, "He would have needed help to get us up to that hotel room."

"Probably the women," Viktor said absently, still wondering how drugging them had netted the bartender five grand and a trip to hell.

"What women?"

"Didn't you check your cell phone this morning?"

Sasha nodded. "Of course."

"Pictures of us in bed with two women, likely high-end sex workers."

"Not on my phone."

A chill skittered over Viktor's spine. This whole thing was supposed to be about setting Sasha up. So why where there only pictures on his phone? "Are you sure?"

Sasha responded. "Da."

Viktor demanded, "Check my phone."

"Where is it?"

"My pocket."

Sasha leaned down and slid his hand into Viktor's back pocket. He couldn't help it. He tensed his ass as Sasha caressed his buttocks.

"Not there. The other one." He hated the breathlessness of his voice. He was in a vulnerable position. The guy could kill him easily. Even though Viktor didn't think that was what was going to happen, if he was wrong…his error in judgment could get him dead.

Sasha reached around to the other pocket, the move bringing him closer. So close that Viktor could see the lust flare in his eyes. Sasha's arm was around him and then his gaze dropped to Viktor's cock again. He throbbed with unrequited anticipation. If Sasha moved much more, his face would be right in Viktor's crotch.

Sasha nuzzled his cock with his nose.

Viktor began to sweat. He wanted this man so damn much.

Sasha's proximity was an exciting aphrodisiac that even the danger circling them couldn't quench. Or maybe he was a sick son of a bitch, and the danger only enhanced the desire fizzing through his veins.

* * *

*S*asha stared at the bulge in Viktor's pants. Heat pulsed off the sexy man. Damn, but he wanted him.

He needed to focus on the bigger problem here. Reluctantly, he slid the phone out of Viktor's back pocket. Instead of rising to his feet, he knelt in front of Viktor. The pose was provocative, submissive. He left himself open to attack and he knew it. However, he hoped that the show of trust would pay off later.

"Password?"

Viktor rattled off six digits. Sasha smirked. He now had intelligence about Viktor.

He rolled his eyes. "I'll change it as soon as you are gone."

Sasha pressed the icon for photos. There were several of him and Viktor in bed with two *prostitutkas*. The way the four of them were positioned made it difficult to see the women's faces. Except in profile.

The camera caught both Viktor and Sasha's faces perfectly. Condom wrappers littered the bed, except there hadn't been any wrappers in the bed with them the next morning. And Sasha did not feel as if he'd had sex.

"Do you know them?" Viktor asked before he could question the same.

"Never seen them before." But Sasha studied the pictures looking for what could be used as kompromat. While the pictures were not optimal, he doubted they would get either of them in trouble. "Any ideas?"

Viktor shook his head. "The women are confusing."

He was right. Incriminating pictures of him in bed with women, even though it looked like an orgy, wasn't enough to cause him problems.

"Is this about you?" Sasha needed to know if this predicament was not even about him. After all, he'd been given intel on Viktor and told to observe him. Maybe more than one agency was watching Viktor. Or maybe someone was setting Viktor up and Sasha was just collateral damage.

Or maybe someone was watching Sasha from within his own agency. *Piz-dets.*

"Those pictures can't harm me." Viktor was frowning at his phone.

Sasha looked at the pictures once again. But instead of focusing on the women, he was drawn to the thick muscular chest with the angel tattoo and the bulging biceps of the man in front of him.

Viktor was hiding something from him. But he couldn't hide his arousal. Sasha was damn sure he wasn't faking.

He set the phone on the floor and placed his hands on Viktor's knees.

Viktor jerked at the unexpected touch. "What are you doing?"

Sasha wasn't sure what he was doing. Touching Viktor was a monumentally bad idea. However, they were alone in his apartment, and it was clean. Sasha had swept for bugs and surveillance devices before Viktor got home.

"I don't know." He shouldn't admit that he wasn't in full control of his faculties. His world was spiraling out of control around him. He prided himself on always being in control and always being one step ahead of the machinations of his government and his targets.

He had been trained in the many aspects of torture. He had also been trained in sensual technique. Sometimes it was better to seduce the truth out of your target rather than use force. But Sasha had always used force.

He slid his palms up Viktor's tense thighs. His muscles bunched beneath his hands. And the bulge in Viktor's pants grew larger.

K chertu eto. Fuck it.

He rose up on his knees and pressed his torso between Viktor's spread thighs. Taking his gaze from the man's impressive cock, he stared at the sharp planes of Viktor's face and studied his ruddy cheeks and the soft huffs of breath. Viktor's eyes burned with lust, but he didn't fight against the restraints. He held still, waiting for Sasha to make the next move.

Sasha popped open the button, unzipped Viktor's jeans,

and reached into the open V. He curled his callused fingers around Viktor's cock, the skin satiny smooth and burning hot beneath his rougher palm. He wanted to melt at the soft glisten of precome on the head.

Sasha rubbed his thumb back and forth over the head of Viktor's cock. The musky scent of arousal permeated the space between them. Sasha's cock surged against his zipper protesting the confines of his tight jeans. His body knew what it wanted, and what it wanted was the man in front of him.

He usually did things like this in the shadows, hidden away, furtive and quick so that he wouldn't get caught.

But strange things were afoot and his life was in flux. Uncertainty cast a shadow on everything. He had no friends, and enemies were everywhere.

Even this man could be his enemy. Sasha had no confirmation that Viktor was exactly what he said he was. Evidence could be faked. Danger could come from any direction. Sasha was tired of always denying his urges, tired of denying his sexuality, tired of denying his very essence.

For once, he'd like to have a sexual encounter that had an honesty of a sorts between him and his lover.

Honesty might be a bit of a stretch, but at least Viktor knew who he was, what he was capable of. The other lovers he'd had did not really know him.

He hadn't allowed himself to get close to anyone besides his mother and she was gone. Even she hadn't known all the things that he'd done in service to Russia and Putin. But Viktor knew him. He knew his job. Viktor knew he was dangerous. If that rocket in his pocket was any indication, he didn't care that he was at Sasha's mercy. Or maybe that turned him on even more.

He shoved his palms around Viktor's butt and pushed his jeans to his thighs. Viktor helped by lifting his hips, so the material slid easily down his legs and bared his straining erection.

"This is a bad idea," Viktor said breathlessly as Sasha lowered his head.

"Da."

He licked that precome off and softly sucked the bulbous head into his mouth. Sasha leaned forward and took Viktor's cock as deep as he could, swallowing, breathing through his nose. Viktor's blond curls teased the tip of his nose as he sucked hard.

There was no finesse as an intense undeniable desire overtook him. He leaned closer, his chest bracketed by Viktor's thighs as he bobbed up and down on the man's cock. Viktor swelled even larger, and Sasha paused, breathing through his nose and trying to slow down.

But when he paused, Viktor surged his hips up and begged, "Harder, dammit."

Ah, Sasha was not going to be directed. And if he went too fast this would be over too soon. Sasha softened his mouth and used his tongue to play. Completely ignoring Viktor's demands.

Viktor's hips surged again, shoving his cock all the way down Sasha's throat. Helplessly he began deep throating him, sucking hard.

Viktor groaned long and hard. "I'm going to—"

Something snapped. Viktor had broken the ties that restrained him. Viktor's hands bracketed Sasha's head, his fingers threaded through his hair.

Sasha knew he should not leave himself defenseless, but he couldn't even bother to care. He'd unzipped his own pants and gripped his cock hard, fisting himself as he deep throated Viktor.

They were both vulnerable to each other right now, but

instead of attack, Viktor jerked Sasha's face into his crotch. "Fuck. Me."

Sasha could feel his orgasm gathering at the base of his spine, his balls tightened up. Keeping one hand on his own cock, he shoved the other beneath Viktor's and pressed his finger along Viktor's perineum.

The move threw Viktor into orgasm. His body bowed in a rictus of pleasure, his head thrown back and his hips pushing into Sasha's face.

Sasha swallowed and swallowed and swallowed Viktor's come. The musky taste poured down his throat and catapulted him into his own orgasm. His come sprayed over the rungs of the chair as he continued to pump away, his cock unbearably sensitive. Viktor had dropped back into the chair and his fingers caressed Sasha's head and neck and shoulders as he eased him through the let down from his orgasm.

The scent of sex surrounded them.

Viktor continued caressing Sasha as his cock softened in his mouth.

Sasha rested his cheek on Viktor's thigh for a moment, suddenly wishing that they could go to bed like a normal couple. Wake up in the morning and have sex, read the paper, and enjoy a cappuccino together.

But his path had been predestined years ago. That kind of life would never be for him.

* * *

While this had been an incredible interlude, a moment out of time, a thick tension settled in his apartment. Viktor tugged his jeans up. Sasha eased back from him and the chair. The sudden swish of air was cold, bringing him back to sanity.

"Why did you do that?" Viktor asked bluntly. He could not figure Sasha out.

Sasha shrugged lazily. "I wanted to."

But that answer was far too glib. This was a man who probably thought out every consequence, every reaction to every action, whose risks were calculated, and every move planned with back up moves and contingencies.

"Aren't you worried that I'll tell someone? That I'll leak this."

Sasha straightened. Studied him. "Will you?"

No. Of course not.

If anything, Viktor felt even more protective of Sasha than he did after the night in the bar. This urge to protect him was… unexpected. However, he wasn't about to share his more tender feelings. "Not at the moment."

"Good." Sasha shifted to his feet, signaling an end to the slightly awkward post blowjob moment. They needed to clean up before they had the next conversation.

The logistics of cleaning up covered his embarrassment. Viktor grabbed a bath towel from his closet and tossed it to Sasha.

Sasha rubbed the towel over his abs and cock. Viktor began to sweat. Jesus, the man was built. His suits hid an incredible body and a physique that must take hours of intense training to maintain. And fuck, Viktor wanted him again. That orgasm had only taken the edge off.

His cock rose, ready for round two. But he couldn't.

At least there were no pictures of just the two of them.

"Your apartment was clean."

Viktor stiffened. "Of course, it was." Now that reality was setting in, he started to get frustrated.

Something was out of whack.

"Sit." They sat at his small kitchen table; there wasn't room in his kitchen for the chairs to be across from each other, so they ended up sitting close.

"Let me see the photos again," Sasha demanded.

Viktor silently handed him his cell. Sasha studied each picture while Viktor studied Sasha and wondered why Sasha didn't have the photos on his phone. "Staged."

Absolutely, they were. "Is this about you?" Viktor asked.

"I don't know," Sasha said. "You could be the target."

Blackmail. Except he already had someone blackmailing him. He wasn't that unlucky, was he? "Doubtful."

Except he didn't really know did he? He needed to talk to Jill again.

"Who do you trust?" Sasha asked.

"My team. My bosses."

Sasha smirked. "Seriously?"

"They have my back."

Sasha shook his head. "Must be nice. You might want to be more careful. Everyone is your enemy."

That comment struck Viktor hard. He was so grateful that he had his friends. "You trust no one?"

"Nyet."

"We need to find those women." He didn't tell Sasha he already had Kita looking into it. No need to play his entire hand. He wasn't completely ready to trust Sasha Loblaw—after all, didn't he just tell Viktor he should trust no one?—but at the moment they were in this together.

"They could easily have been paid through an app and have no idea."

"True, but it will be another piece of the puzzle." They could trace the user who had paid them. If Sasha couldn't trace the money paid to the bartender, then the sex workers were likely another avenue. "Cash is less traceable."

"However, they don't seem to be completely worried about

tracing if they paid the bartender in a wire transfer." Sasha tapped the table, clearly thinking things through. Viktor noticed his lean fingers and strong wrists.

"Those women are likely in danger." Viktor wasn't responsible for Mack's death, but he could still feel bad about it. His murder added another layer to the deepening mystery.

Frustration rolled from Sasha. Not only the women could be in danger. Self-preservation indicated that he and Sasha were in danger too. But from whom? And why?

"Da. I can't use my resources at the embassy," Sasha ground out. He frowned as if thinking about something unpleasant.

"My coworker can do some digging." No need to tell Sasha he'd already sicced Kita on this. He thought about his shirt and the lipstick on the collar. "I might have some DNA."

"How?" Sasha demanded.

"Lipstick on my shirt." Why hadn't he thought of that sooner? Because he hadn't thought that he would need to. This morning, tracking down DNA seemed like overkill.

"I have someone who could analyze it," Sasha said.

Their brains worked in sync as brainstormed their next course of action, seamlessly feeding off each other. This felt like they were a team. A team with one person holding back. Viktor shoved away his guilt. He had to assume Sasha was keeping things from him as well.

A partnership based on lies. His stomach grinded.

"We're agreed about next steps." Viktor wanted some assurance from Sasha that they were on the same page.

"Da." Sasha stood. "Give me the shirt and I'll drop off with my contact now."

Viktor headed for the hamper in his bedroom. All thoughts of sexy times disappeared when he opened the lid.

"Fuck."

"What's wrong?"

Someone had accessed his apartment and stolen the evidence. Things were adding up to a very ugly picture. One Viktor didn't like at all.

"My clothes are gone."

Chapter 9

---

*V*iktor met the Cigarette Man on a bench near the Lincoln Memorial Reflecting Pool.

The man was in disguise, wearing a dark wig, mustache, fake eyebrows, thick black glasses, a jaunty fedora, and a long caramel-colored pea coat. He still wore those damn scuffed shoes.

Cigarette Man had avoided Jill's attempts to get in touch before finally calling Viktor and arranging a meet between Christmas and the new year.

He was surprised the man hadn't come back to the ALIAS offices, instead he'd requested a meeting here. Viktor would have preferred this meeting with Jill, but she was in Scotland. Viktor told Jill where he was going and who he was meeting with. Her response was to make sure Viktor knew that he didn't have to do anything the guy asked.

But Viktor had questions. Lots of questions.

Kita was still running programs to find the women but it was a slow process hampered by the fact that they only had partials and side views.

The lab had gotten back to him, but the results of the blood test were inconclusive. He'd been roofied with a generic date rape drug that was pretty much untraceable.

Viktor pressed the record button on his phone.

"Did you or your agency have something to do with the Mack Garcia's death?"

"I didn't kill anyone." He was very emphatic. Cigarette Man also didn't seem all that upset about the bartender's demise, and he didn't ask who Mack was, so he gave away the fact that he'd known about the bartender. "My understanding is accidental overdose."

Bullshit.

"Were you having me followed?" Because Viktor hadn't intended to do more than observe the night he'd met Sasha.

"Unimportant." Cigarette Man dismissed his question.

"You never mentioned that you planned to drug me."

"We needed pictures. The means were left up to the individual."

"The individual as in Mack the bartender?"

He shrugged. "No idea."

Then his words hit. *We?* "Is someone else involved?"

"You completed my request. You got him in a compromising situation. That is all that matters to me." He crossed his ankle over his knee, his foot bobbing.

Viktor didn't like the guy's attitude.

"Why pictures with women?" Viktor pressed. "That won't compromise Loblaw." He forced himself not to use Sasha's more informal first name. He didn't want to give away that he felt comfortable with the assassin. And he absolutely didn't want this man to know that they had interaction after the night of the drugging.

"It's not my place to ask questions. Just like you, I follow orders." But that felt like a cop out.

"Do you actually have the authority to control the narrative around ALIAS?"

At that, Cigarette Man bristled. "I will uphold my end of the deal. I have plenty of clout."

"How do I know you aren't lying?" The man clearly didn't like Viktor challenging his authority.

"I am very good at my job," he insisted. "Adams-Larsen would do well to remember that I hold the advantage here."

There was something off about this whole exchange. "We can weather more bad publicity." But he still felt guilty. Because some of their bad publicity was his fault.

"But now you won't have to." There was a smugness to the man that set Viktor on edge, but he couldn't identify why. He was the ultimate in bland, unassuming, government guy.

Viktor pushed. "What happens now?"

"Nothing." The man smiled, oily and insincere. Just looking at him made Viktor feel dirty.

There had been little in the press recently about ALIAS. The holidays had taken over most of the news with heartwarming stories about donations to food banks and billionaires paying off layaways at Walmart. But now that the new year was coming, Viktor was concerned that the stories would ramp up again. Whether he liked it or not, he had to do everything in his power to protect ALIAS and his friends.

"So Adams-Larsen is clear?" he asked defiantly. After all this, he better come through with his offer.

The man inclined his head.

Viktor wanted verbal confirmation. "I'd like an actual response."

"Adams-Larsen is off the hook." There was something in the guy's tone that set Viktor's intuition humming. An insinuation that left him hanging. Because he hadn't said that Viktor was safe. As if the guy wasn't done with him yet.

Viktor wanted to ask about Sasha. Wanted the confirmation that he hadn't somehow set Sasha up for more grief. Wanted to know what they were planning for him next. He felt sick that he'd helped Cigarette Man. And he couldn't risk this man understanding that he and Sasha were more than passing acquaintances. How much more was still up for debate.

"Who do you work for?" Viktor wanted to know.

"Unimportant." Cigarette Man brushed aside his demand and Viktor wasn't in a position to press him. "I'll be in touch."

"I thought we were done."

"*We* are." He was smug, as if he knew a secret.

"I'd say it was a pleasure, but I'd be lying."

As he walked away, Viktor couldn't help but feel unsettled. He didn't think he'd seen the last of Cigarette Man.

* * *

Sasha entered the embassy for his daily report at the appointed time. He nodded to the guards and headed for the conference room that was comparable to a US Intelligence SCIF, a shielded room that could not be spied upon, no windows, and soundproofed walls, to make his secure encrypted video call.

"You left something out of your report last week." The ambassador's impassive face and arctic voice filled his video screen. No hello. No warm greeting.

Sasha had filed his daily reports with some careful editing. However, he knew he needed to stay close to the truth since he was being watched. He'd tagged several people following him over the past few days. He'd ditched them when he went to Viktor's, but otherwise he let them trail him doing mundane things like going to the grocery store and the drug store.

"What are you speaking of?" But a frigid cold had invaded

his body. Because the only way his superior would know he'd left something off was if he'd been followed.

"You went to the bartender's apartment."

"Da." He was pissed, but he didn't show it, keeping his voice even. "He was dead—which I put in my report. There was no point in adding that I went to his domicile. I was more than careful, and I searched for anything that could tie him back to me and the embassy. There was nothing."

"Did you kill him?" the ambassador asked.

"Nyet." Sasha shrugged. "That would be stupid."

The ambassador studied him. Nodded.

Sasha raised an eyebrow. "Is there a reason you're having me followed?" He went on the offensive rather than playing defense. It was fishing, pure and simple. He'd tagged several different operatives. Could one of them have killed the bartender? But why?

There had been no cameras at the bartender's and he'd watched the building before entering. Which meant that he was being monitored. Had someone followed him to Viktor's? Because that encounter, he'd definitely left out of his report.

He'd been very careful. He'd left his official phone at his apartment. He had taken precautions, but if someone had somehow seen him at Viktor's, that could be a problem.

Because he was being so closely observed, he'd given Viktor a burner phone with only one number in it. Sasha's burner. He wanted to see him. Badly. But that would be dangerous for both of them.

"This case is very important. I have more than one operative working it. You apparently crossed paths."

Sasha didn't believe that for an instant.

He had always believed in the greater good. Protecting Russia, his motherland and his people. A silent warrior who did the hard things so that others could be safe, but recently he had awoken to the realization that he had been used, his loyalty misplaced, his patriotism a tool to be wielded against him.

So he'd done the unthinkable and become an agent for the US government. But they weren't much better than Russia. He understood that.

Both governments saw him as expendable.

Now if his actions were to be discovered, he would be done away with just like the many he had taken down in the name of protecting Russia. The irony wasn't lost on him.

He didn't want to die.

In fact, he wanted to live. Many would say that he'd done more than his share of living in his forty odd years. He'd traveled all over the world in his job, seen many cultures and societies, and had always believed that Russia was superior… until he hadn't.

For many years, he had disdained the United States. He'd mocked their insistence that they were the best nation in the world, their political correctness and their cancel culture and their obsession with morality, but at least people like him had the chance to live their lives.

He was under no illusions. The American government was using him too. But they, at least, shouldn't be out to kill him.

He had information, years of memories of events and actions that Russia had taken in the US, years of intelligence he could share with the US government. He possessed a list of Russian-sponsored assassinations performed in the United States in his brain. Information the American intelligence agencies might suspect but could never confirm.

He also wasn't stupid. He had been dribbling that that information out slowly, in digital dead drops, so they continued to pay him. He also knew that if Russia discovered that he was selling information, he would be dead. Even if the

US found out that the Russians knew, the Americans would not intervene. He was on his own.

Besides, they would not want him to defect. They would want to keep using him for information against Russia. He was done.

Too many leaks. Too many people in the intelligence community would sell him out for the money or the recognition.

He was on his own.

His heart thumped as he realized that his years of service meant nothing. All the things he'd done in service to the Kremlin, to the FSB, to Putin, to preserve the status quo were dust in the wind.

Rather than rage at the ambassador and tip his hand, he asked calmly, "Any information on who did kill the bartender?" It had been over a week since Sasha had found the man.

"That line of intelligence is dead."

No fucking kidding. Mack had expired in a long slow wheeze of breath after the drug suppressed the ability to breathe, blood pressure dropped, and pulse weakened, heart in cardiac arrest.

"Is there another avenue you wish me to follow?"

"Keep on Kuznets," the ambassador ordered. "I still think he could be the traitor."

"I found no evidence to suggest he is working for either government." Viktor had been a medic in the army, after several years of service, he'd been posted at the CIA through some sort of joint sharing program. That's believed to be where he met Kita Kim, who then convinced him to follow her to Adams-Larsen.

Where he worked...doing something that was a whole lot more mysterious than image consulting. Perhaps security for their clients. There was no question he was proficient with weapons. His entire life had been in service of others. The polar opposite of Sasha.

The deeper things went, the more Sasha thought that Viktor was merely a pawn in a larger operation. An unsuspecting pawn, at that. He'd seemed genuinely distressed that the bartender was dead, even though the man had drugged them.

"He is very…American." Truth. Justice and the American Way. He was a veritable Boy Scout.

The temptation of Viktor was a liability. His attraction to Viktor could get them both killed.

Yet he still couldn't stop fantasizing about him. He couldn't stop picturing Viktor's perfect lips sucking his cock while he deep throated him. Sasha had been jacking off to the fantasy every night.

Blyad, he shouldn't be thinking about blowjobs while on a call with his boss.

"Why did you go to these places?" The ambassador gestured to Sasha's most recent report. Sasha had done reconnaissance on the Adams-Larsen offices and a few other places in DC.

"Trying to re-trace Polzin's steps. See where else he went. Looking for connections between them all."

"You are supposed to be surveilling Kuznets."

"I met with him." Sasha couldn't figure out why his boss was pushing him on Viktor. "We discussed Polzin and he agreed to inform me if he discovered anything else about Polzin's mission."

Ambassador Dubov waved away his comments. "Polzin is a dead end. I've been informed that he had been meeting a lover. Not selling weapons."

"That tracks." Sasha answered, "Kuznets had no information on weapons sales. It's in my report."

"Any aftereffects from being drugged?"

"Nyet." He felt fine.

"Any chance of kompromat that could be used against you?"

"No one has approached me." He had left out the fact that Viktor had also been drugged. He also didn't reveal that Viktor had pictures of them with *prostitutkas* on his phone. He wanted Viktor off Dubov's radar and any retaliation that the ambassador might dream up.

"*Prevoskhodno!*" Excellent. "I have not heard any rumblings either." Dubov directed him, "Keep digging. We have a traitor, and we need to find them. Otherwise, we will give them this Kuznets to pacify them while we search."

Manufacture evidence to make Viktor the traitor? Yes, that had been his intent when he'd first been given this assignment and Viktor's life was of no consequence to Sasha. But now he could not let that happen.

Sasha needed to come up with a traitor. *Bystro.*

* * *

*V*iktor headed to Jillian's office. He'd wanted to wait to approach her until he potentially had some leads to follow up on. But now all he had was more questions.

"Come."

"Welcome back." He closed the door softly. "How was Scotland?"

"Wonderful." She smiled, her mouth softening into satisfied grin.

He was glad for her. She deserved some happiness. He

hated to destroy her good mood but this really couldn't wait any longer.

"What's wrong?"

"Several things." Viktor hesitated. Things were coming at him fast and furious, spinning out of control. "Sasha came to see me last week."

Jill stood so fast her chair nearly tipped over. "What?" Her gaze skimmed over him. "You're okay?"

"I can take care of myself." He should feel slightly insulted. Except, she cared.

"I know. But you're aware of his reputation."

Which meant Jill had done some digging of her own.

"Yes." Sasha carried an aura of brutality. But Viktor had also seen a different side of him. "And I have no doubt that most of it is true."

"What happened?"

"We had both concluded that the bartender is the one who slipped us the drug."

"Okay." Jill rubbed her hands together. "Let's follow up with the bartender."

"Can't." Viktor paced. "He's dead."

"Dead," Jill said flatly.

"'Accidental.'" He put the word in air quotes. "Overdose."

"Did Loblaw do it?"

"I don't believe so."

His boss's mouth tightened. "Why don't you suspect Loblaw?"

He shouldn't say that it was his gut. But it was his gut. "He seemed genuinely surprised."

Viktor paused, realized his gut wasn't enough. He thought about the file he had on Loblaw and his own extra research. He tried never to go into any situation blind.

"Besides, that's not his style. He'd be more likely to slit his throat up close and personal so everyone would know the man was murdered. The FSB relies on their enemies knowing that they won't hesitate to kill them if they fall out of line."

If rumors were correct, Sasha didn't have a signature, per se, but he delivered death quickly and painlessly. Mack Garcia's overdose would have been painful and messy. That was not Sasha's style.

"Good point."

He relaxed when Jillian agreed.

"Cigarette Man said he didn't kill Mack."

"Then who did?" Jill pulled a ball of yarn and some knitting needles from her desk drawer. "Maybe the bartender was supposed to do more than drug you."

Viktor hadn't considered that option. Both he and Sasha had been at someone's mercy. Yet the worst that had been done to them was some compromising pictures and waking up together.

"So…you two got cozy?"

He blushed. There was no way she could know about what happened in his apartment. "We compared notes. And agreed to share intel." But he couldn't share the most important fact, that he'd had a hand in Sasha's set up. "I did not tell him about Cigarette Man."

He couldn't reconcile why the photos were only on his phone.

"Why?"

"Why would Cigarette Man have pictures of us taken with women?" Viktor questioned. "Besides, Sasha didn't know about the pictures. They weren't on his phone."

Jill frowned as she carefully knit a circle of blush pink yarn, the beginnings of a cap for one of her favorite charitable organizations. Something was off about the whole situation. "Have you looked for the women?"

"Kita found one. She's still looking for the other."

"Can you interview her?"

She must have seen the truth on his face.

"Dammit." Jill slammed her knitting needles down on her desk. "Did she die the same way?"

Viktor shook his head. "Bludgeoned to death." Whoever had killed her had worked out some serious rage. Multiple fractures. Her face had been swollen and disfigured and discolored from purpling contusions. Her death had been violent and brutal.

"Anything in the coroner's report about weapon?" Jill asked.

"Still waiting on the final report, but preliminary report said blunt force trauma, using an object with some sort of ridges on it." Viktor stalled for a moment.

"What's wrong?"

"Whoever took the pictures may have taken my telescoping tactical baton." Viktor's stomach gurgled. Could they have used his weapon to kill the woman?

That became a fuck ton more problematic for him.

"If those marks were made by your baton…" Jill picked up her knitting again. "…then someone set you up."

But no one had come for him. He'd been extra careful since being drugged. "That would be my assumption."

"What the hell is going on?"

"Can we trust Cigarette Man?"

"He works for the government." Jill's knitting needles clacked together as she furiously knit, then purled. "But we all know that our government is run by people who are human and motivated by things other than duty and honor."

"Do you think he had her killed?"

"I can't…imagine that that was sanctioned, on US soil." Jill continued to knit furiously. "I'm not naïve enough to think that the US has never engaged in state-sponsored killings…but in DC? And over a potential intelligence source that may not even be willing? That just doesn't make any sense."

"Especially in this method."

Jill pursed her lips. "Was there evidence of sexual assault?"

"I'll have Kita check the final autopsy report when it is released." He wasn't quite sure where she got the photos. And he wasn't about to ask. He didn't want to get her in trouble.

"None of this adds up to convincing a potential target to spy for the US. So what is really going on?"

The dead bodies were piling up. Viktor couldn't help but think that the Cigarette Man was lying to him. So far the only evidence of that night was on Viktor's phone. Not Sasha's.

"What agency does he work for?"

"The less you know, the better."

Except was that true? Not knowing anything was unsettling. "He promised that my job was completed, and that ALIAS was off the hook."

In theory they could drop this and pretend it was over.

"We're not going to let this go. We'll keep digging until we get to the bottom of this," Jill said. "People are dying."

And every new revelation was not good for Viktor. So he would like to know what they were up against.

When had he started thinking about Sasha and himself as a they? Grouping them together was dangerous. Sasha had said it. He wasn't trustworthy. No one was.

"Maybe I can figure out what they really want so we can stop anyone else from getting killed." Namely him or Sasha. And the other missing woman.

But frankly, he couldn't stop thinking about Sasha with his mouth wrapped around his dick and wishing he could return the favor. He wanted to explore that connection between them that seemed to grow stronger every time they met.

Jill rubbed her hand over the back of her neck. "I'm sorry I got you into this."

He waved away he apology. "I would do anything for you." They hadn't always been as close, but recently she'd become more like a big sister to him. And he meant it. He would protect Jill, Kita, Marsh, and everyone else at ALIAS with his life. Because they had his back when his family didn't.

"You shouldn't have to," she said vehemently.

"Maybe not." *But let's face it.* "Life isn't always fair."

Chapter 10

*I*t was time to stop fucking around.

Viktor headed toward the address he'd obtained for Sasha. He had no idea what was happening. He didn't like so many unknowns. He needed some answers.

Especially after Kita got the final autopsy report on the call girl.

He'd been tempted to use the burner phone but he wanted to talk to the man in person.

He let himself in to a modest apartment building in Alexandria, Virginia. The old building had been converted into condos a few years ago. They'd kept a lot of the period features from the turn of the century building: tall baseboards and ornate molding, heavy wooden doors, slanted wood floors, and granite and marble fireplaces.

The building owners had upgraded the exterior security features, new double-paned windows and steel exterior doors. Enhanced measures to access individual floors, with keys needed to access the stairwells and elevator. No doorman or human guards. If there were security cameras anywhere but the exterior corners and over the entrances, they'd been very well hidden.

Fortunately, Viktor had a universal key typically reserved for fire and police departments...and if that didn't work, he also had heavy-duty lock picks.

Sasha's apartment was in a residential neighborhood on the fourth floor, difficult to access from the exterior but not impossible. Likely so that if the spy needed an alternate exit, he could climb out his windows and down the side of the building.

Viktor strode up to Sasha's apartment and knocked. He had no intention of hiding his presence, but he sure would like to take Sasha by surprise.

No answer.

He waited a minute, then knocked again. He glanced up and down the hallway, searching for more surveillance devices, but didn't see any.

Viktor used the universal key to unlock the door.

Way too easy.

He slid inside the apartment and waited for an attack. But the air was eerily still. Nothing moved. He closed the door. "Hello?"

He paused to the side of the doorframe and leaned back against the wall to study the interior of the apartment. Clean lines with modern furniture, a single sofa, a television perched on a credenza, heavy velvet drapes that could be pulled closed but weren't. Books on the built-in shelves.

In the kitchen, the refrigerator hummed quietly. He took stock of the contents. Condiments, a bottle of orange juice, a leftover container from a restaurant, several bottles of vodka and frozen dinners in the freezer. A glass, small plate, and utensils were in a dish drainer on the counter to the right of the old enamel sink. A half full bottle of wine sat on a trivet. A stack of paper napkins and a single placemat sat on the table. A rolling cart in the corner under the window held a microwave.

The atmosphere was stale and the whole place felt abandoned. A hint of bleach scented the bathroom. A barely squeezed tube of toothpaste rested on the counter next to the sink, shampoo on a shelf in the shower, and a single towel hung over the rack. He sniffed at the towel. There was a hint of Sasha in the cotton, but not enough of his scent if the man had showered here recently.

Viktor wandered into the bedroom, but he already knew he'd find nothing.

This wasn't where Sasha Loblaw *lived*. It was a decoy.

Viktor assumed that if it was a diversion to throw pursuers off the track, Sasha was watching or had surveillance on it.

Viktor wandered back into the living area and studied the books. There were a variety of books from Russian history, American history, biographies, and spy novels. He seemed particularly fond of John Le Carré.

Viktor removed a book on the Cold War and settled on the sofa. He propped his feet on the scarred rectangular coffee table, flicked on the small lamp and began to read.

* * *

*W*hat *was Viktor Kuznets up to?*

Sasha watched the man settle into his sofa as if he belonged there. When the alarm had gone off, indicating that someone had breached his fake address, he'd been curious and hoping he'd find out which FSB operative was closing in on him. No one from work knew he had a separate address. The move was fairly new. As soon as he decided to put his plans in motion, he'd stopped living at his official apartment.

When he'd seen Viktor on the feed streaming to his laptop from the small cameras set up at his apartment, his initial thought was that he'd been wrong about the man. That sharp stab of disappointment had taken him by surprise. He didn't want to be wrong about Viktor. He wanted the man to be innocent. Sasha hadn't been *innocent* for a very long time.

He wanted Viktor to be guiltless with a naïveté that took him by surprise.

He hadn't thought he had any raw, youthful fantasies left. They had been beaten out of him after years of violence and brutality. But Viktor seemed to pull this dangerous gullibility from him.

He hadn't been able to stop thinking about Viktor after their explosive sexual encounter. He'd relived those moments every night, his own cock in hand. If he were another man, in another universe, in another circumstance, he might be able to pursue a relationship with Viktor. He liked him.

He'd left him the burner phone and half hoped that Viktor would call just to talk.

They'd had an entertaining and riveting conversation in the bar before they'd been drugged. But a life with a man, an American, was never to be Sasha's fate. After all, he was going to have to disappear soon. Either that or he would die.

In the meantime, he needed to know what the hell Viktor was doing.

He picked up his burner phone and dialed.

The phone rang. Sasha watched the monitor as Viktor pulled out the cell Sasha had given him. "Yes?"

"What the hell are you doing?"

"Waiting." *For your call* was implied. Sasha noticed that Viktor didn't say anything that would reveal who he was talking to or what they were talking about.

"What if I'm not the only one watching?"

Sasha watched the screen as Viktor frowned. Tilted his head. "You think this is a possibility?"

He was thankful Viktor had censored his words.

Sasha had suspected that his fake apartment had been under surveillance by his superiors for some time. The fact that he'd been attacked in the Metro station on his way home from the embassy earlier indicated that they had gone from surveillance to attack.

"You should get out of there," he said abruptly.

"Where should I go?" Viktor raised an eyebrow and smirked straight at the camera. The man knew his electronics.

"Home."

He shook his head. "I need to discuss a matter with you, and it should be done in person."

Sasha shouldn't be alone with him again. For multiple reasons.

If Viktor saw Sasha now, there would be questions that he'd prefer not to answer. He was still coming to grips with his situation.

He meant to say go home again; instead, he found himself rattling off his address. "Take precautions." He swept for bugs regularly, but he couldn't guarantee there were no bugs in his decoy apartment. But he was still concerned especially since he could not confirm that Dmitri was not following him. And what if the ambassador had ordered additional surveillance on Viktor and not told Sasha?

The ambassador had no compunction about ordering the death of an innocent man if it furthered his agenda.

Viktor rolled his eyes. "Not an idiot."

Sasha knew that. "I don't want you to get hurt." The words burst from him, without permission, revealing far more than he had intended.

The lines of tension around Viktor's mouth softened and his lips curved into a smile. "I'll be fine. Nice talking to you."

And the waiting began.

Sasha paced the confines of his living space. His actual, secret address was only across the street from the decoy, but true to his word, Viktor didn't arrive for another thirty minutes.

Finally, a sharp thump sounded as Viktor knocked on the door.

Sasha peered through the security peephole, knowing that if Viktor was followed that he had jeopardized their safety. He yanked the door open, standing behind solid wood. "Come in."

Viktor sauntered into Sasha's apartment without turning around. Walking as if he owned the place. His confidence was sexy as hell.

Sasha shut the door quickly. "You weren't followed?"

"Give me some credit."

Viktor surveyed his surroundings in a sweeping glance taking in the bright modern furniture, clean lines, and the black-and-white photography on the walls. "This place suits you."

He decorated with free rein in his personal space. In public, he was quiet, unobtrusive. He blended into background, an inanimate statue that people's gazes skimmed over. A nothing bodyguard that no one noticed.

In his own space, he favored bold colors, bright furnishings, an in-your-face vivacity and lack of compromise, to brighten his mood after long, dark days.

Viktor pivoted and gasped. "What the fuck happened to your face?"

"I had an unfortunate mishap on a Metro platform."

"A *mishap* like the guy last week?" Viktor brushed a gentle hand over the darkening bruise on Sasha's cheek.

Last week's "accident" had been ruled a suicide.

But Sasha knew a hit when he saw one. The man in question had been posting anonymous blogs criticizing Putin and the oligarchs raking in the cash while average, everyday Russians scrimped by on substandard wages. The US-born man had worked for several ultra-wealthy Russian billionaires in Miami before quitting and hiding in DC.

Today's attempt had been similar. Someone had shoved him, endeavoring to push Sasha onto the electric third rail in the Metro station. But Sasha had honed his survival instincts over many years. He'd known he was being followed. He'd lured his pursuer to that particular station.

Just as the man struck, Sasha shifted, and the assassin overbalanced and fell onto the tracks. But he'd grabbed for Sasha and ended up shoving him into the wall.

"He is no longer a threat."

He had fried on the train tracks. Sasha escaped through the maze of tunnels connected to the station, avoiding the regular exits in case the assassin was working as a team—which was possible. But the incident underscored that Sasha didn't have much time left. He should be angry about the attempt on his life, but he was mostly accepting. His time was almost up. However, he couldn't die until he'd protected Viktor.

Viktor studied him, searching for something. Sasha had no idea what he wanted to see.

"I am...glad you are okay," Viktor finally said.

"You need to watch out yourself."

"Are you threatening me?"

He wasn't so far gone that he could admit to Viktor that the Kremlin had him in their sights, but he needed Viktor to understand that he was in danger. "Nyet."

Viktor walked over to one of his early works, a black-and-white photograph of a turbulent sky over the Potomac. He'd altered the photo to add a slash of red through the storm clouds. Viktor's gaze slipped to the bottom corner where typically an artist would sign. It was blank.

Viktor turned to Sasha. "This is you?"

Sasha shrugged.

He continued to study Sasha's photos. No one ever visited his sanctuary because no one knew it existed.

When the ambassador was in residence, Sasha frequently stayed at the official Russian residence. This place was an indulgence. A gross use of money the US government was paying him that he should be funneling toward his retirement. But he'd needed the space, the tranquility of silence that came with this sanctuary. The stark white walls and the bold splashes of color from his photos were his way to focus when his world was closing in on him.

"What makes you think it's my work?" He found it fascinating and alluring that Viktor recognized Sasha was capable of beauty.

Viktor moved around the room slowly, studying each photo as if he'd be quizzed on them later. "You have an exquisite eye for composition."

Sasha shrugged, inordinately pleased. Looking through a viewfinder wasn't that different from a sniper scope. He'd found a refuge in using his skills to create beautiful photographs. A way to balance out the karmic scales, beauty to counter death.

"You going to tell me why you are here?" Because if they were seen together, it would be bad for them both.

Viktor shook his head and didn't answer. He took another minute to survey the surroundings. Sasha was sure he also made note of the weapons hidden in plain sight. "Cameras?"

"Not in my private home."

Viktor pulled a small device out of his pocket, flicked it on, and prowled the perimeter of the room. Twice.

But the green light never turned red.

"Are you done?" Sasha said drily.

"Cannot be too careful." Viktor's gaze skimmed over him. "For all I know, you record everything that happens here."

Chapter 11

"**W**hy are you here?"

"I found one of the women."

Grim lines bracketed Viktor's perfect mouth. It was the closest he came to betraying any agitation. His hair was moussed and sculpted into clean lines, his jeans and long-sleeve shirt were pressed and neatly tucked in.

Sasha already suspected the answer, but he asked anyway. "Dead?"

"Yes."

Fuck. Sasha wanted to slam his fist into something. "Pictures?"

Viktor reached into his compact backpack and pulled out a manila folder. "She was found in a hotel room at the Hay-Adams."

Viktor handed Sasha the photos and their fingertips brushed against each other. A shiver worked its way through his body, sizzling along his nerve endings like an electrical live wire, sending pulses to his brain and his cock.

He studied the dead woman dispassionately. His gut churned like a ship tossed about on the waves. Someone was going to a lot of trouble to tie up loose ends pertaining to him and Viktor.

Why? There had been no communication from anyone regarding the photos.

"Has anyone contacted you about the pictures on your phone?"

"No."

"Any idea what game these people are playing?"

"Not really a game." Viktor's gaze cut to the gory photograph, lingered there. "Two people are dead. And another is missing."

Sasha wasn't prone to fear—far from it—but a flicker began in his belly.

Something about Viktor's refusal to meet Sasha's gaze sent another warning blaring in his skull. Viktor knew more than he was telling. He should be more worried about what he was keeping from him, but Sasha would admit, only in the confines of his own mind, that he was happy to see him.

He couldn't afford to be happy.

"Cause of death?"

"Appears to be beaten to death."

"Appears to be?" Sasha didn't like where this was headed.

"Actual cause of death was a single puncture wound likely caused by a sharp knife which pierced the heart. She bled to death internally. The beating was either to obscure the cause or someone takes a lot of pride in disfiguring and obliterating for shits and giggles."

Blyad.

Sasha studied the details in the photos. This murder was not the same as the bartender. The overdose wasn't a quick, painless killing.

She died from the knife blade. The beating was overkill.

The woman's execution, however, gave away her murderer.

His heart iced. Dmitri Komarov's signature was a single death wound and then he beat the body severely. Sasha knew it well. He'd cautioned him, again and again, when he'd been training him, not to leave any tells, any characteristics for authorities to connect his kills. But the man's ego would not be appeased.

Like the meaning of his surname, the little gnat had been a pest in Sasha's side since the day he'd begun to train him. Clearly, Dmitri had continued to carve his signature in his jobs. Sasha had been adamant that one day that egotistical need to mark the kill as his was going to be his downfall.

Someone was bound to notice and connect the dots.

And the FSB did not take kindly to obvious evidence.

If his compatriot had killed the woman, then something more sinister was going on. Because it meant a concerted operation to either frame Sasha or compile evidence to indicate he was no longer fit for his job.

He thought about the look on Viktor's face, the hesitations, the fact that he'd been put in this man's path, and that everything had focused on Sasha interacting with Viktor.

Maybe Viktor was involved in whatever plot had been hatched?

Maybe everything that had happened since they had met had been orchestrated.

He'd never let anyone in his true apartment. He had evidence that could bring down the ambassador and cause significant harm to US-Russian relations if the public got wind of the assassinations performed on US soil.

In Russia, these deaths, enemies of the state, were sanctioned directly by Putin and the government. But the US took a dim view of state-sponsored assassinations on home territory.

His final ace in the hole was the information in his head. If Dubov or his bosses at the FSB knew he intended to share it with the US government, it was no wonder they wanted him dead.

If they knew he had a bolt-hole apartment but couldn't get inside, maybe Viktor was his honey trap.

In a violent burst of movement, he grabbed Viktor, spun him, and pinned him against the wall. Sasha had positioned the man so that he could observe his facial expressions in the entryway mirror while he questioned him. Even though he'd planned on this apartment being his refuge, he'd still decorated in such a way that he could observe the entry from multiple vantage points.

Sasha disarmed Viktor, removing a knife from an ankle holster and a tactical pen from his shirt pocket. He pushed into Viktor's muscular back, his cock nestled against the man's rounded buttocks, and his member rose in tribute.

Viktor didn't fight, didn't cower. Which confused the hell out of Sasha.

"Why aren't you afraid of me?" Sasha was used to people approaching him with a level of fear. Even people who didn't know him felt fear in their very essence when they came into contact with him. Yet, this man, this upstart didn't back down. He didn't back away. His response was so very intriguing. "Most people are."

He met Viktor's gaze in the mirror.

"I...don't know," Viktor replied, seemingly just as confused as Sasha by his lack of fear.

He nudged him harder against the wall. "You should be."

"I'm aware." He rubbed his buttocks against Sasha's growing erection. "But your soul calls to me."

"That is illogical." But he felt it too. This connection that seemed to grow deeper every time they interacted.

"You won't hurt me. I know this deep inside." Viktor

dropped his forehead to the wall and breathed deep. "I am not afraid. I am aroused."

Viktor's breath had quickened, his chest rising and falling in slow, measured rhythm as if he were forcing himself to stay in control.

"This is not rational. This thing between us defies common sense," Sasha argued as he held his need to nuzzle the man's ear in check.

Viktor laughed. "You are correct. But lust is never logical, is it?"

"I don't understand." Sasha shifted his hips, rocking involuntarily against Viktor's ass.

"You lie."

Sasha stiffened against him.

"Any man who can take photographs with such passion, with such longing, understands what I am talking about," Viktor said softly. "How did you survive working for the FSB for so many years?"

Sasha leaned closer to Viktor, nuzzled his nose against the shell of his ear, and then licked. His chest was pressed against the sculpted muscle of Viktor's back. Heat rose from the places their bodies touched.

Viktor's breath caught.

His smell, an earthy soap and pine deodorant, was intoxicating. "You are more luscious than an entire vat of vodka."

Viktor trembled. "Of course I am. Vodka is disgusting."

* * *

S asha barked out a laugh.

His chest shook with the force of his amusement and bumped against Viktor's back. It was taking everything

Viktor had not to fight to break Sasha's hold. He really didn't think Sasha would hurt him—if he was wrong, it could be his death—but he also chafed at the submissive pose.

He knew that Sasha needed to feel in control. He understood that need. Especially with everything else spiraling out of control. Sasha had recognized something in those photos.

He knew that Sasha also felt this overwhelming attraction. But he had a hell of a lot more to lose if they indulged.

"Did the FSB send you?"

The shift from sexy to interrogator was jarring. But Viktor frowned. "You think your bosses sent me?"

"Da. To tempt me." His mouth pinched closed.

"No. I wasn't sent by your bosses." Viktor swallowed. He couldn't tell Sasha about the Cigarette Man. He couldn't put his coworkers in jeopardy. But he could try to reassure Sasha that Viktor wasn't being manipulated by the very people who *should* protect him. "I give my word."

Sasha appeared to relax. "*Khorosho.*" Okay.

This was already no casual encounter or furtive, transient tryst. They knew things about each other.

Viktor turned his head so that his cheek rested against the wall. His erection jabbed the wall as if trying to punch a hole in the plaster. Sasha's breath was hot, and the warm caress of his tongue along the tendon in his neck was oddly erotic.

They really shouldn't do this. But oh, did Viktor want to. "You're playing with fire," he cautioned Sasha. On too many levels to acknowledge.

Sasha slid one palm down Viktor's stomach and over the material of his jeans, cupped the head of his cock in his palm. "I'm playing with *you.*"

Sasha ran his nose along Viktor's jaw, and he fought back a moan.

They had more important things to discuss. But Viktor couldn't concentrate on anything but the man at his back and how much he wanted him. He was vulnerable. He'd done enough research on Sasha to understand that the man could snap his neck in a heartbeat.

He felt on a visceral, fathomless level that Sasha wasn't going to hurt him. At least not physically. That level of trust was shocking. Completely unexpected.

Although if Sasha ever found out about Cigarette Man that could change. Viktor had no doubt that Sasha would be ruthless if threatened.

They needed to talk about what was happening. "We really should discuss—"

"How much I want to fuck you."

Viktor jerked as his body flooded with arousal, his brain releasing chemicals to ramp up his desire. All the air in the room disappeared in a torrent of lust. His heart bumped at a rapid pace, his muscles tightened, and his ball sac drew closer to his body, preparing for sex.

All thoughts of talk evaporated.

"Take off your clothes," Sasha demanded.

Viktor's heart thundered. The past few days he'd been on edge. His brain had returned again and again to the memory of Sasha going down on him in his apartment. Of Sasha naked in the shower. Of Sasha smiling at him over a drink.

The longing to connect with him, physically, mentally, emotionally was strong.

He was lonely.

He'd been avoiding his co-workers because he couldn't tell them about the Cigarette Man and his threats. Luckily it had been fairly easy because it was the holidays, and everyone was busy with their families.

But Viktor had had no one to spend the season with.

He had no intention of betraying his friends. But this wasn't a betrayal. Unlike the last time, Viktor had what Sasha wanted. Not the other way around.

"Only if you take yours off as well."

He turned around to face Sasha, studied his black eye. He wanted to tear off Sasha's clothes and examine every inch of his body for other injuries.

There had been so much in Sasha's statement. Someone had tried to take him out. Gratitude that Sasha could more than handle himself welled up inside Viktor.

"I am so very glad you are okay." He gently kissed the edge of Sasha's black eye. His heart clenched at the thought that he could be looking at another set of photos. Pictures of a dead Sasha. "I can't imagine a world without you in it."

Sasha's eyes flickered, a trickle of warning buzzed in Viktor's brain. The concern flitted away when Sasha diverted Viktor's attention. He curled his fingers in Viktor's waistband and slowly popped the button his jeans.

Viktor's fingers trembled as he unbuttoned his blue cotton shirt. Sasha lowered Viktor's zipper with agonizing care, his cock nearly busting the zipper in its eagerness to arrow toward the man.

"Don't stop." Viktor groaned when Sasha wrapped his hand around Viktor and squeezed.

He shrugged out of his shirt and stepped out of his jeans, leaving them in a pile on the floor. Desperate to be naked.

Then he lifted Sasha's shirt gently over his head, taking care with his body. Sasha shoved his pants and underwear down to his ankles with little finesse, leaving him naked. "I wouldn't miss this."

Sasha leaned forward, pressing Viktor up against the wall. Sasha rubbed his cock along Viktor's. His desire surged at the hard caress. Sasha bent his head and licked Viktor's tattoo, tracing the angel wings with his tongue. Viktor curled his arms around Sasha's waist and yanked him closer, caressing the smooth skin of Sasha's back, and learning the contours of his muscles. The hot suction of Sasha's mouth against his skin raised goose bumps and his nipples hardened as Sasha used his teeth to nip at him.

Viktor groaned, already so hard his cock was painfully full.

He scraped his fingers up Sasha's neck and tunneled into his hair at the base of his skull, cupping his jaw in his hands. He bent his head to kiss the man who had haunted his dreams. "I want you so fucking much."

Viktor couldn't keep the kiss light; he needed to devour him. To inhale his essence and take it inside. Sasha angled his head and attacked, rocking his hips against Viktor's as they dueled with mouths, and lips and tongues.

"You can have me." Sasha growled.

Lust ripped through him with claws, tearing down his walls and leaving him open for love. This wasn't about loneliness. This insatiable need to possess was about a connection that went beyond attraction, beyond desire to something deeper. Something primal.

As if Viktor's body recognized Sasha on some fundamental level, some alternate plane of reality where they could be together forever.

Chapter 12

Viktor woke quickly, realizing immediately he wasn't in his own bed. He lay on his stomach, his erection pressing into the silky cotton. He sensed the presence next to him and turned his head to stare at his lover.

Last night, he'd explored every inch of the man. His scars, his muscles, investigating every hollow and earthy hidden erogenous zone.

Sasha's smooth cotton sheets were supple and sensual against Viktor's skin. They were an unexpected luxury. Although everything about Sasha was becoming unexpected. He'd been a generous and creative lover. The best Viktor had ever had.

Viktor's stomach churned because he was still deceiving him. He knew that Sasha wouldn't take kindly to that fact if he ever found out.

Sasha rolled out of bed in a burst of movement, crouching next to the bed, mimicking the first time they woke up together.

Viktor pushed to sitting, leaning against the tufted fabric

headboard, arms across his chest, as he skimmed his gaze over Sasha's body.

Sasha's cock arrowed toward him, and Viktor's mouth watered.

"What are you doing?"

"Not used to waking up with someone." Sasha stood fully, rubbing his palm over his hair. If Viktor wasn't mistaken, the man was embarrassed.

He liked the fact that Sasha wasn't used to sharing his bed.

The first time, he hadn't been able to touch, but this time, he planned to take full advantage of the fact that he was free to caress him, to trace every bone and muscle of Sasha's body, to love him as he needed to be loved.

Viktor's cock tented the silky sheets. Sasha's gaze dropped and he licked his lips as if remembering the first blowjob he'd given him.

Everything about their first sexual encounter had been erotic, forbidden. "While I loved it...."

"Me too." Sasha's grin was cocky.

Now was Viktor's chance to suck his lover's cock. "Not this time."

It was time for Viktor to take control. Viktor curled his fingers in a come hither gesture. "Come closer."

"Make me."

Viktor got to his knees and curled his palms around Sasha's taut butt and pulled him to his mouth. "I want to suck your dick." He kissed the tip, tonguing him hard.

"That works," Sasha said breathlessly.

* * *

$\mathcal{S}$asha lay on his back, his chest rising and falling rapidly. A sheen of sweat covered his body, his scent rising from the heat between the two of them. Viktor trailed his fingers lazily over Sasha's pectoral muscles, then flicked his nipple.

Sasha grabbed his hand and threaded their fingers together. "We need to talk."

The past hours in bed together had been amazing. Spending the night with Sasha had been liberating. Sharing pleasure with Sasha had been life changing.

"Playtime is over?" Viktor recognized the necessity, and he still mourned the fact that the next few moments were going to be unpleasant. He'd have liked a little more time to revel in the afterglow of sex. To bury his head in the sand and pretend that someone wasn't gunning for one, or both, of them. Viktor was beginning to think it was both.

"We can't delay any longer."

They each had ties to what was happening. Viktor had a choice to make. How much did he share with his lover? Maybe he needed to see how much Sasha was willing to share with him.

"What did you recognize in the photos?" Viktor's stomach churned.

"The signature."

The signature indicated some sort of pattern or routine that a killer always used when he or she committed murder. "Someone you know?"

"Someone I trained." Sasha turned his angry gaze on him.

Betrayal.

Viktor tiptoed carefully through the next question. "Do you think he was acting on his own?"

Sasha was silent so long, Viktor thought maybe he wouldn't answer. But finally he confessed, "I don't believe so."

"Someone is setting you up?"

"Possibly."

Even though Viktor knew it was a possibility, Sasha's answer sent a dagger through his heart.

"You said that you recognized his signature…won't others do the same?"

"If he's acting on the orders of someone higher up, it won't matter." Sasha tilted his chin toward the ceiling. "The fact that he used the signature tells me it was a great big fuck-you to me."

"Can you tell me his name?" Viktor's brain was racing. Was there a way they could alert the authorities to his identity?

"You need to steer clear of this man. He is dangerous." Sasha squeezed his fingers.

"I'm not planning on catching lunch with him."

"This is not the time to joke."

"I understand." Viktor couldn't help but push. "But maybe I can get the authorities to look into him."

"He's got diplomatic immunity," Sasha said.

"Please."

Sasha was silent for so long, Viktor wondered if he would ever answer.

"Fine. Dmitri Komarov."

Viktor nodded. "So he likes to kill quickly and then beat them while they bleed to death internally?"

"He doesn't like blood."

Viktor shuddered. "I can understand that."

"But you are a medic. Nyet?"

"Doesn't mean I like blood." Viktor shrugged away his embarrassing response to medical problems. "What does he use to beat them?"

"He is adept at improvising," Sasha continued. "He likes to use something on site that cannot be tied back to him."

Viktor froze.

He never had found his tactical baton.

"What's wrong?"

"I was carrying a small tactical baton the night we met. It was gone the next morning."

Could the set-up include Viktor? Could Dmitri have been behind the pictures with the sex workers?

Except that was orchestrated by Cigarette Man. Right?

"We need to find that baton," Sasha said grimly.

"We?" Viktor blew out a breath. He lay on his side, his head propped in his hand, their legs tangled together.

"Da. We are in this together." If that admission made Sasha uncomfortable, he still wasn't trying to get away from Viktor. That was a thrill. It meant that he trusted Viktor too. That this...thing between them was *between them* and not one-sided strictly on Viktor's part.

Viktor trailed his fingers lazily back and forth over Sasha's chest, dipping his fingers onto his low belly, watching as Sasha's cock responded, even though they'd just finished a marathon of sex. "I like your apartment."

"*Spasibo.*"

That wasn't all he liked. But he likely wasn't special. A stab of jealousy cramped his gut. "Do you bring many people here?"

"Fishing, *dorogoy*?" Sasha chuckled.

Viktor liked the term of affection just a little too much. But he decided honesty was the best way to go. "Yes," Viktor admitted.

"No one."

He stopped his nervous fidgeting. "Really?"

"I am the product of a Russian upbringing and the tutelage

of the FSB," Sasha said drily. "This kind of interaction is frowned upon."

"And yet here we are." Viktor thought perhaps he was missing something important. "So you don't bring…anyone home with you?"

"I do not engage in dalliances."

"I'm a dalliance?" He wasn't sure how he felt about that.

"Nyet."

"But—"

"You are more." Sasha's palm was solid against his, like a promise. "Against all reason. Likely to my detriment…and probably my downfall."

Viktor stiffened.

"Don't say that." A cold fear settled in his gut. "Are you worried about the assassin?"

"Dmitri? Pfft." Sasha shrugged away the concern. "Can I beat him? Da. Will I be able to without repercussions? Let's just say I should stay away from open windows and speeding trains for the moment."

Viktor shuddered and held on to Sasha more tightly. He felt an uncontrollable urge to shield him.

"What are you doing?" There was an unexpected amusement glimmering in Sasha's brown eyes.

"I find myself wanting to protect you," Viktor confessed.

"You know I am a feared assassin, da?"

"I know who you are." He stared him straight in the eyes daring the dangerous man to look away. "Do you?"

* * *

"Do not romanticize me." Sasha's mouth tightened, and he looked away. He loved the adoration in the younger man's eyes, but it was misplaced. His gut twisted. "I am not worthy of that hero worship."

Viktor snorted. "I prefer to think of you as a sex slave."

Sasha laughed, his belly rippling with the force of his amusement. "I like that much better than hero."

Viktor asked, "How did you come to work for the FSB? A violent past? A taste for killing? How did you catch the eye of the Kremlin?"

"I was…a brawler when I was a kid. I had to be to secure food for my mother and me. My father died in a skirmish in Afghanistan during the Soviet-Afghan war." At least, that is what they had been told. With Russia, one never knew what the truth was.

"I am sorry about your father."

"I never knew him." Sasha shrugged. He'd been searching for a father figure for years. "When I was a teen, they made me an offer I could not refuse."

He'd been ready to fight to protect his mother. But then they'd enticed him with visions of money and safety. And his mother would be taken care of. How could he turn that down?

Viktor waited.

"They gave my mother a good life. A better life than she would have had if I'd had not agreed."

Gave? Not exactly but close enough.

"So you did everything to protect your mother."

He spit out, "I enjoyed the luxury, the clothes, the cars, the travel. I was a poor kid from *Moskva* who got to see the world." His stomach twisted again.

"Who wouldn't? Especially if you came from nothing."

"Less than nothing." He could admit that he didn't want to give up the finer things he'd grown accustomed to. But he was tired of the violence, the constant on guard and worry, the ever-present pressure that it could all be taken away.

Now it appeared perhaps they were getting ready to take it away. Whether he was ready or not.

"Where is your mother now?"

Sasha stiffened, looked away, the grief in his heart like a slow heavy drumbeat. "Dead."

"I am sorry."

He didn't want to talk about his mama. Didn't want to bring the fury at his country, at his circumstances, into this bed with his lover. His body readied to fight and he knew that Viktor could see his rage.

"I'm angry." He couldn't help the words that burst from him.

Viktor responded with a caress. "Why?"

"They wouldn't let me go see her before she died." Sasha clenched his hands into hard fists. "After everything I've done, I just wanted to say goodbye to my mama. And they took that from me." He could feel his rage bubbling to the surface. He wanted to hit something.

"I'm sorry they did that to you."

"You are estranged from your parents."

Sasha could tell Viktor didn't want to answer, but he relented.

"Yes." He didn't ask how Sasha knew.

"Why?"

"Turns out they were okay with me being…" He waved his hand between their two naked bodies. "As long as I hid it and didn't tell anyone…I was tired of hiding."

Sasha could understand that. "What is it like?"

"What?"

The longing that filled his heart expanded. What would he give up? What would he become in order to be free? It had never even been a consideration. Until now. The idea was so big he could barely imagine it. "The freedom to be who you are. To be with who you want to be?"

"Well, currently it isn't very freeing." Viktor skimmed his palm over Sasha's shoulder and pressed a kiss to the curve between his neck and shoulder. Goose bumps pebbled his skin and his heart thumped. "As my lover is forbidden."

"How do you feel about that?"

"I'll take this...whatever we can have." Viktor pressed a line of kisses along his jaw. "For now."

Sasha wanted forever. But that was more than a wish it was an impossibility.

However, maybe they could spend the day in bed. Take this moment out of time and enjoy each other.

But then Viktor said, "I need to go soon."

"Why?"

"I volunteer at a local homeless shelter." Viktor hesitated. "It's busy this time of year. American holidays are difficult times."

Sasha wanted to know everything about his temporary lover. "Why there?"

"My family was homeless when we first arrived in America."

Sasha stroked his hair, waiting because clearly there was more to the story.

"My father was angry when he realized that the American dream wasn't the easy process he'd been led to believe."

Sasha continued to wait.

"We spent the first year here bouncing from shelter to shelter," Viktor said. "To repay the kind people who took care of us when we first arrived, I try to volunteer a few times a month. After all, I am blessed with abundance now."

Sasha had seen his apartment. Abundance was a stretch. "You are a good man."

"Not that good." Viktor skimmed his palm over Sasha's abs and reached for his erect cock. His grip was firm, a little rough, as he pumped Sasha. He tightened his fingers and quickened his strokes.

Sasha placed his hand over Viktor's. "Slower."

He had a man, a man he really liked, in his bed. He wanted to savor these moments. To revel in the luxury of sex that wasn't furtive and rushed.

Viktor stared deep into his eyes. The fathomless well of lust, overlaid with something that felt like...affection, shimmered in his gaze. Sasha's heart thumped.

Viktor had a hold of his body. But Sasha wanted to hold this man's heart.

He cupped Viktor's jaw in his hands, tracing the sharp lines of his face and skimming over his lips. He lowered his head and whispered against his mouth, "You are my reward for this life I've lived."

Viktor placed his hand over Sasha's heart.

"We are all works in progress," Viktor said. "Perhaps your life will take you in a new direction. Perhaps one day..." He trailed off. There was so much hope in his voice that Sasha knew he was destined to be disappointed. "There will be a chance for us."

He spoke the forbidden out loud.

But neither one of them believed that.

"People like me don't get to move on."

Distress crossed Viktor's face, warming Sasha. He cared.

"Then you'd better make the best of right here and right now." Viktor wrapped his arm around Sasha's neck and pulled him closer.

"You are the best of here and now." Sasha breathed him in and held his essence in his lungs, wishing that they had tomorrows instead of just today.

"Show me."

* * *

*V*iktor needed to go.

He'd lingered far too long in Sasha's bed. But the fear that this was all they might have had kept him here instead of preparing to leave.

Viktor had dressed and gathered his belongings. He hated to leave but he wouldn't go back on his promises.

"Tell me something," Sasha said.

Viktor tensed, because Sasha had lost his teasing affection and there was a seriousness to him now. "If I can."

"What does Adams-Larsen really do?"

"I don't know what you mean." His heart thumped. Because of course he did.

"I have done research on you." Sasha propped his head on his hand, his elbow digging in to the bed and his biceps bunched. He was still naked in the bed and using it as a distraction. "I know you are more than an image consulting firm."

"What makes you say that?" Viktor tried to deflect.

Sasha just looked at him. "We could start with your obsession with weapons."

"Obsession." Viktor laughed. "Hardly an obsession."

"How often do you need your shuriken while fixing a politician's parking ticket problem?" Sasha shot back.

Viktor sighed. He wasn't wrong.

"I noticed that there were several whispered instances of your clients disappearing." Sasha pushed to sitting. "Did you make them disappear?" He put *disappear* in finger quotes.

"You think we killed people?" Shock buzzed Viktor's chest like the zap of a Taser set to a very low voltage.

"Nyet. You are too much of a Boy Scout," Sasha teased.

But Viktor thought there was a question in there. He didn't know how to respond. Guilt that he was hiding things from Sasha coursed through him. "Sometimes we give our clients who are in danger a little cover just until they are safe." Of course, the truth was far more complicated than that, but Viktor couldn't divulge what they really did. "We help with their social media."

Sasha said, "Pfft. Americans and their need to document their every move for strangers."

"Agree, but it's a problem these days." Viktor tried to give him information that wouldn't get him in trouble. "We protect their privacy." All things they did, just with a little extra.

"So…you don't fake people's deaths?" Sasha asked lazily. Tension shimmered in his muscles. "Someone like say…Sergei Polzin?"

"What?" Viktor laughed. "Is that a rumor going around? That we faked Polzin's death?"

Sasha relaxed. "Perhaps."

Apparently, Sasha knew when to use silence to his advantage. Viktor finally couldn't stand it. He wasn't giving away ALIAS secrets by denying this.

"No. We don't fake someone's death," Viktor said. "Everything we do is legal and above board."

"Ah, no breaking the rules then?"

"No." Viktor shook his head vehemently. "We protect people who need help."

"It is good to know that you had nothing to do with Sergei's death."

A cold wave of trepidation spread through Sagh Viktor at the way Sasha said that. As if he'd closed a bullet point on a job, a task he could now check it off.

"That's a matter of public record."

"Mostly," Sasha said arrogantly, "But there is no information on who shot Sergei, so my superiors thought maybe he didn't really get shot."

"Is that why you had sex with me?" Viktor stood rooted to the floor, unable to move. "To find out if I'd somehow, what? Hidden Sergei Polzin in a safe room in my office for the past few months?"

Sasha shrugged one bare muscled shoulder. "It was a pleasurable way to gather intelligence."

That fantasy Viktor had been building in his mind, a place where he and Sasha could be together, could deepen the connection that already existed, crumbled in the face of Sasha's words.

Ha. What connection? Sasha was telling him in so few words, that everything he'd thought about their attraction was fake. An operation to spy. How could he have been so stupid?

To be duped again.

Chapter 13

$\mathcal{H}$is time was running out.

Sasha had to give the Kremlin a traitor—not Viktor—so he could disappear. Before they discovered that he had a relationship with Viktor.

Sending Viktor away had been hard. He had wanted to spend the day in bed, linger with his lover. But the more time they spent together, the more danger Viktor was in.

Watching the hope in Viktor's gaze turn to hurt had been devastating. Better to nip Viktor's attraction before he became even more difficult to give up.

Sasha had planned this visit carefully. He prepared his official report to the FSB on the assassination of the prostitute making sure to indicate in his official report that Dmitri had used his signature and that it could be a problem for them. Using the report as an excuse, he went to the embassy. He would have to take evasive maneuvers to get there without getting attacked.

He also added an addendum about the recent heart attack death of a suspected double agent. The death had been ruled an accident. But he knew that the FSB had been killing dissidents and other enemies of the state for years without detection.

He'd been part of that killing squad.

Unfortunately, earlier in his career he hadn't kept records. He'd been loyal. But he remembered every man and woman that he had eliminated. Now he was recreating those records and sharing that information with the US government. Even without proof, the CIA would have intelligence on Russia.

He didn't think he'd been discovered by the FSB…yet.

The recent attacks on him could be warnings. But he knew that if they found out he was the traitor they were looking for he was dead. Unless he disappeared. And maybe not even then. But he was going to try.

If he went down, he was taking as many with him as possible.

Now it was time to go on the offensive. Dmitri had grown up in the Tambovskaya Bratva and then joined the FSB. The fine line between the state sponsored security and the bratva was very thin. But in true Russian standards, the government was the greater of the two evils.

Sending Viktor away had been easy to accomplish. Twisting that figurative knife in Viktor's heart had cut out his own. He'd been able to hide his distress. Fortunately, Viktor had been so upset that he hadn't noticed that Sasha was dying on the inside.

He'd had to get rid of Viktor. To save him. Viktor needed to stay far away from Sasha. And he had made that happen.

When he was quizzing Viktor about Adams-Larsen, he'd held out hope that he would have another option. That hope, maybe there was a way out, was crushed by Viktor's denial. He needed to finish his "investigation." He also needed to know how many agents were assigned to him right now.

His life was a tragedy that just kept on getting worse.

Had he become a target of a hit squad like the URPO operation? As far as Sasha knew, the assassination project had been shut down.

At least he'd been told it had been. If there was evidence that the project had been reinstated or continued, there was only one place that the information would be stored.

He was going to have to break into the ambassador's safe in his private sitting room.

Sasha had worn his suit into the office as he always did. He bowed his head at the two security men at the ready at the door. "Vasily. Vlad."

The two men, armed with AK-47s, nodded to Sasha. "Good morning."

Sasha swiped his badge to enter the interior offices of the embassy and headed for their secure room to transmit his report. He booted up his secure laptop and opened a connection to the ambassador.

"Loblaw." The ambassador tilted his head. "Problem?"

Sasha wasn't going to back away. "Not anymore."

The ambassador's eyes flinched, giving him away.

"Did you send Mikhail to kill me?" That was who he tossed onto the third rail.

"Nyet." The ambassador was lying. Sasha had identified his tells over the years.

"Do you have any idea who did?" Sasha kept his tone hard. "And why?"

"Perhaps the traitor has found out you are looking for him."

A convenient excuse. "Possible."

"Have you found him?"

"Nyet." Sasha rubbed his mouth. "Do you have any intelligence on what agency he is giving the information to?"

He needed to probe. "Or what operations they are leaking to the Americans? Perhaps if I had that information, I could narrow things down."

"What about Kuznets?"

Sasha kept his face impassive. "As far as my investigation, I've found nothing to suggest that he is involved in the espionage community at all. I hate to waste time on a dead end."

"But someone like him is the perfect person to extort influence over."

"Someone like him?"

"*Gomik.*" The ambassador spat the word as if a curse.

"True." Sasha grimaced.

"Abomination." The ambassador glanced over his shoulder and appeared to duck, as if dodging an enemy.

"I will continue digging."

"I must find and eliminate this traitor." Ambassador Dubov's hands trembled. "Or the Kremlin will send me back to Moscow."

Sasha was confused. "I thought you wanted to return to Russia."

"Not anymore." The ambassador eyed him somberly. "It is better for my family if I stay in the United States."

Suddenly, things made more sense.

The ambassador signed off, but Sasha covered his camera and stayed signed on. He left his phone on his desk, and started a recording of standard office noises, closing doors, tapping fingers, keys on the laptop clacking, then he snuck down the corridor and entered the ambassador's office. He glanced around, making sure there were no new cameras. He pressed the book, Tolstoy's *War and Peace*, and the paneled wall slid open revealing a passageway. He headed into the secret tunnel that connected the ambassador's residence with the embassy and ran.

The distance between the two buildings was about two miles. Sasha sprinted the entire way.

Once he arrived at the ambassador's secret entrance, he ran a scanner over the door to the residence, then pressed the code to open the door. No one was here. The ornately-decorated mansion was deserted while the ambassador was gone. No one entered the mansion, not even the cleaning staff, when the ambassador was visiting their home country.

His paranoia worked in Sasha's favor. He kept close to the walls as he skirted around the first floor, then headed to the private sitting room where he'd sipped tea not long ago. Sasha had kept the knowledge of the safe, hidden behind the painting, a secret for fifteen years. He hoped the ambassador was as lazy about changing this password as he was about other security details. The ambassador assumed that his personal safe, in his private residence, was not susceptible to hacking or intrusion by an enemy.

Sasha tried the old combination. But nothing happened.

No click, no tick indicating the safe had opened.

Sasha thought about the prior password, which was the date the ambassador was appointed to this embassy. He tried several other significant dates in the ambassador's current tenancy, but nothing opened the safe.

He needed to hurry. The recording only had a few minutes before it began repeating. If someone was listening, they might realize he was no longer inside.

In desperation, Sasha entered the ambassador's son's birthdate. And finally, the safe opened. The safe was full of money and jewels. At the very back was what looked like a perfume bottle in a clear Plexiglas box. Except Sasha knew this was no Chanel No. 5.

Sasha's blood ran cold.

The ambassador had a toxin in his safe, likely something developed at the state-run poison factory outside of Moscow. They did not use these toxins in the US. In Europe they had great success putting it on light bulbs and doorknobs, and even a teapot with Litvinenko and several others. But the backlash from using the deadly substances had paused that program. Now they used more traditional methods, train accidents, falling out of a window accidently, or toxins that mimicked heart attacks or even some that grew a slow cancer, so it would take several painful months for the victim to die rather than radioactive polonium like they had used on Litvinenko.

Sasha took a picture of the bottle. He couldn't take it with him even if he wanted to.

Sasha ignored the toxin in favor of the files. From his pocket, he pulled out a scanner that resembled a ballpoint pen and opened the files so he could copy them. He glanced at the simple watch on his wrist. He didn't have much time.

When he opened the final file folder, his heart stopped. In the back of his mind, he'd held out a small hope that maybe his employer wasn't trying to kill him.

But there it was in black and white.

Not only were they trying to kill him, but they'd ordered multiple agents to try. And they'd put the order in writing. Almost unheard of.

He had a giant target on his back.

* * *

*V*iktor rode the Metro to get to his shift at the homeless shelter.

He volunteered on weekend mornings doing what he

could to help with intake and convince people that they would be safe at the shelter. Sometimes he did a double shift, the shelter and then the food bank. There, he helped sort donated bags of food so the different types of cans, boxes and containers could be warehoused together. But occasionally he drove the forklift when they received pallets of fresh produce or donations from manufacturers.

Whatever he did was some small way to give back for the times he and his family had been taken care of by the shelter. His father had been too proud, until his mother begged. They'd been cold and hungry. His father had worked two jobs and they still hadn't had enough for both food and a place to live. It had always seemed as if they one but not the other.

He sat on the train, in the last car and the last seat in the car, facing the rest of the passengers. One part of his brain kept track of the riders, searching for anyone suspicious. Because this was his routine, he thought it necessary to stick to it. He would have preferred to spend the day in bed with Sasha. At least until Sasha had gutted him with his confession that their interactions had been a lie. Then all he'd wanted was to go home and wallow in regret.

But it was the holidays, and the shelter was going to be busy. This was a rough time of year, and he wasn't about to leave those in need in the lurch.

His brain kept returning to last evening…and this morning. And then the way Sasha had basically shoved him out the door with the admission that he used sex to get information from Viktor.

He fought the urge to frown.

There was a lot fucked up about this whole situation. He had been thrilled with their growing closeness, until Sasha had burned it to the ground.

A pall spread over him. He had wanted fiercely to tell Sasha about Cigarette Man and the plot to set him up. But if he did, he'd be betraying Jillian and everyone else at ALIAS. He was trapped between his friends and his lover.

He still felt slightly guilty that he hadn't shared with Sasha that the US government wanted to recruit him.

Except his lover had no idea.

And apparently his lover had been playing him the whole time. Thank God he hadn't revealed that the Cigarette Man was trying to set up kompromat to recruit him as a spy.

Even after the way Sasha gutted him, he still worried about him. About his "accident" in the Metro, likely from his own people, and the threat of the Cigarette Man's trap.

An older homeless man got on the train, his gray hair a nest of dreads and wood beads, his ratty trench coat hung on his frame, overly large for the man's body.

But as he shuffled toward the back of the train, toward him, Viktor's gaze sharpened. His shoes were shiny except for that one scuff. Son of a bitch. What was he doing here?

Viktor sighed and slid over. "Wouldn't have pegged you for a Metro rider."

The Cigarette Man said, "You have anything for me?"

"A lot of questions." Viktor wasn't about to give this guy any intelligence regarding Sasha. Did that make him a chump? Maybe.

"I can't answer them."

Viktor wondered what this guy's deal was. And what was he really after? "Can't or won't?"

"Both." The man rubbed at that spot on his shoe. "Did you get any more that I can use?"

"I thought you said we were done?"

"Is anyone ever really done?"

He didn't like so much about this.

"Are you sure there isn't anything else I can use?"

Viktor might be upset with Sasha, but he wasn't going to give this man any intel that he didn't have to. He'd done what the guy had asked. "No. Did you kill the woman?"

Viktor had scoured his apartment again for the baton, worry that someone had used his weapon to kill her.

"Of course not." But he knew about her death. That was clear from his shrug. As the train slowed for the next exit, the man said, "Keep working him."

There was a desperate tinge to his voice that elevated Viktor's concern. Why was this guy so insistent? He knew enough about intelligence to know that not every op was successful. It was a numbers game.

"He isn't interested." Viktor denied their attraction. It felt like a betrayal. Even with the fact that the man had all but shoved him out of his apartment this morning.

The man snuffled. "You sure?"

Viktor tried to deflect but the guy kept pushing him.

"I tried. But he isn't interested in meeting up again." Viktor lied without an ounce of remorse. "Maybe your intelligence about him was wrong. You might try a woman."

His stomach turned at the thought of Sasha with a woman. Which was stupid—he knew that Sasha had sex with women. In his research the man had been linked with several gorgeous women. He'd had sex with them. Viktor had no doubt.

Cigarette Man grunted. "I'll be in touch."

Ugh. Definitely not what Viktor wanted. "Don't bother."

As soon as the guy exited the train, though, more worries invaded. How did the Cigarette Man know he'd be on that train?

* * *

K ita had found the other woman. She'd texted Viktor after he had returned from his shift at the homeless shelter.

He'd waffled between anger at Sasha and worry for him. Especially after the Cigarette Man had made contact with him on the train. His heart hadn't been in the right place to work at the shelter today. All he had wanted was to go back to his apartment and wallow in worry. But first they needed to save the woman.

Maybe when they saved her they would learn who hired her.

Because Viktor was worried that whatever was happening wasn't over. Sasha was in danger.

He'd appreciated the heads-up from Kita. Now he needed to go question the woman and get her somewhere safe. Because if they had been able to find her, whoever killed the other sex worker would not be far behind.

If Sasha hadn't been such a dick this morning, Viktor might have let him in on the interrogation, but he had no plans to include him now.

The woman was hiding out at a seedy motel in a rundown part of town. The exact opposite of the high-end lodging where she had entrapped Viktor and Sasha.

He would need help retrieving her.

Viktor called Jake Brown. Jake and Viktor had formed a bond early on. He was the only other local employee at ALIAS who didn't have any family nearby. Unless he was on date, doubtful this time of year, he'd be available.

"Yo. Vik. What's up?"

"I need a favor."

"You got it." No hesitation. No questions asked.

"It's a delicate matter."

Jake snorted. "In our line of work, what isn't?"

"We need to exfil a woman from a motel and hide her."

"I'll get my bag."

An hour later, Jake and Viktor met up at the motel on the edge of a seedy area of town. They'd taken separate cars and after spending an hour driving around to make sure they didn't have tails, they headed to the motel.

They'd communicated on burner cells, just to be safe.

"Follow my lead." Viktor requested.

"Okay. What do I need to know?"

"I need to scare some answers out of her before we move her."

"What?!"

"It's important." People were dead. He couldn't be a nice guy.

He had Jake knock on the door since she would recognize Viktor.

But she didn't answer.

"Ma'am." Jake pulled out his southern manners. "Hotel security."

"Go away."

"Ma'am, I need to speak with you about a suspicious person in the parking lot."

As soon as she cracked the door, Viktor shoved his foot in and muscled into the room. This woman could have done much worse than drug him. He'd been at her mercy. She could have killed him. And he wanted to know why.

She backed up, cowering as soon as she saw Viktor's face. Saw the rage he couldn't contain.

"I see you recognize me."

"I d-d-don't know what you mean."

Jake shut the door and lounged in front of it so she couldn't leave. She cringed away from him, clearly afraid of the large Black man. Viktor knew Jake would hate that.

"Cut the shit." Viktor slashed his hand. "Who hired you?"

"I don't know his name." She paced the tight confines of the worn motel room. "He's hired me in the past for things." She shot a furtive look at him.

"What kinds of things?"

"Most of my clients are high-end. Guys who want to cheat on their uptight religious wives with a threesome. Or even just to get a blowjob."

"Does he always have you take pictures?" It was a shot in the dark.

She flushed. "Sometimes."

So it had only been the two women.

Jake hadn't said a word, but he'd given Viktor a *what the fuck, man?* look. After all, she had the wrong equipment for Viktor. Everyone in the ALIAS office knew it.

Nervously she clasped her arms around her waist. "Okay, yes. Frequently."

"You realize he is blackmailing them."

She shrugged. "I may have seen one or two of my clients on the news."

"What about me?" Viktor growled, his rage growing. "Do you normally drug men?"

"I didn't drug anyone."

"You had to have known that we were impaired," Viktor snarled. "Are your marks normally drugged?"

"No!" She shook her head so hard her lanky hair swung and hit her cheeks. "He said it was a prank."

"How much?"

She whispered, "Five thousand."

"A prank," Viktor said flatly. "That's certainly an expensive *prank.*"

Jake continued to stand by the door and look menacing. But Viktor could feel the confusion rolling off him.

Viktor asked, "Did we have sex?"

"No." She licked her lips nervously. "We just took the pictures and um, undressed you, and left."

"You didn't think that was odd?"

"I thought it was an easy night," she shot back.

"What were we drugged with?"

"I have no idea!" she cried. "I told you I had nothing to do with the drugging."

"Who did it?"

"I don't know."

"I think it was the bartender." Viktor glared at her.

"Why don't you ask him what he gave you?" *And leave me alone* was implied.

"I can't. He's dead."

She flinched.

"It was just supposed to be an easy way to make some cash." She shivered, her eyes filling with tears. "But then Shanae was found...."

"Beaten to death." Viktor tossed the picture of the other woman onto the scratched and dented dresser.

He wanted her to see the violence. It wouldn't matter if the other woman was killed almost instantly by the knife in the heart. The result was the same. She was dead.

The woman gagged and bent over a garbage can and puked until she was dry heaving. "I thought someone was following me." She wiped her mouth with a shaking hand.

"So you bolted."

"Listen, I wasn't about to stick around and get beat to

death." Her more refined accent disappeared. "I don't know what I'm fixin' to do."

But Viktor was wondering about his telescoping baton. It was still missing. "Did you take anything from me?"

"What? No!"

Viktor couldn't afford to take her at her word. He clenched his fists and loomed over her. She shrank away from him.

He felt bad because he knew that Jake's trigger was violence against women, but Viktor needed her to believe he would hurt her. He shot a look at Jake. "You want to wait outside?"

It was impressive to watch as Jake made himself seem bigger. He hadn't moved and he suddenly took up more space and menace rolled off him in a potent wave. But he was glaring at Viktor.

"Not leaving," Jake said.

"As you wish."

Jake was eyeing Viktor suspiciously. He had to know that Viktor wouldn't hurt the woman. Didn't he? But the woman didn't need to know that Viktor was basically harmless.

She edged closer to Jake.

"Who was the target?" And why pictures with women? He just didn't get it.

"I don't know. I just know if the first attempt failed, we were supposed to get you both into the hotel room and get pictures."

"First attempt?" What first attempt?

"Yes!"

"Who ran the first attempt?"

"I don't know." Her mascara ran down her face smearing over her cheeks.

If the original trap was for both of them, the first attempt could only be the bartender. Right? No one else had approached them.

Except, if they had gone willingly with the bartender, the blackmail would be easy and irrefutable. And a threesome with men.

But once the bartender had figured out that they were not going to take him up on his interest, he must have decided to drug them.

But that was stupid on his part. They figured out quickly that Mack had been the one to drug them. Which was likely why he was dead.

"Can you tell me how you communicate with the man who hired you?"

She wiped her mouth, her eyes scared and bruised. "I can't."

"Can't?" Viktor questioned. "Or won't?"

"I'll never work again if I do."

"You'll never work again if you're dead."

She gasped and made a run for the door.

Jake pulled her back gently and held on to her. "We aren't going to hurt you."

But she was terrified, gasping for breath and hyperventilating. Nothing they said was going to calm her down as she struggled against Jake's hold.

Viktor pulled out a syringe.

The woman squealed.

"Dude." Jake backed up a step. "What the hell?"

"It's just to calm her down."

The woman's eyes widened, the whites stark in her face. And then her eyes rolled back in her head and she went limp.

"We need to get her in the car before she regains consciousness." Viktor was cold, analytical.

"We need to have a serious talk." Jake's voice shook. "This was not cool."

Before Viktor could apologize the door burst open.

Sasha stood in the doorway.

Fuck. Things just went from crazy to batshit insane.

"What are *you* doing here?" Viktor snarled at his lover.

Chapter 14

"*I* see you found her."

Sasha swayed in the doorway, his head swimming. Viktor's image wavered splitting in two then coalescing back into one.

Viktor glared at him as if he'd like to punch him. Too late. Already done. Sasha couldn't blame him. He'd been awful the last time they had been together.

He should have just left this rundown motel when he'd realized Viktor was here.

Seeing him again was difficult.

Wanting who he could never have just drove home how lonely he was.

But after the latest attack at another Metro station, he knew he had to track down the remaining woman and see if he could get any kind of intelligence from her. He hated to keep having to kill his compatriots, even if they were trying to kill him first.

The Black man holding the woman glanced between the two of them with an avid curiosity. "Want to introduce me to your friend?"

"It's better if you don't know who I am." Sasha directed the response to the man since Viktor hadn't said anything else.

"This is Sasha," Viktor finally said, then sent a chin lift. "Jake."

"Is he the other guy?" Jake asked.

Viktor shifted closer to the woman. "What other guy?"

"The one she set up." Jake tipped his head toward the unconscious woman.

Sasha raised his eyebrows at Viktor. "Did she give you any information?"

"Yes," he bit out. "The women were a backup plan."

Well, that made more sense.

"Any information on who hired her?" Because Sasha had discovered after reading through the file, it was not the FSB. They had hired the bartender and subsequently killed him, but there was no evidence that they hired the women. Which meant there was another player.

"No." Viktor ran his fingers through his blond hair. "She became hysterical."

"She's a dead end," Sasha said with disgust. *Piz-dets.* He needed some answers.

"Not if I can help it," Viktor replied.

"Let her go." Sasha's stomach curdled. The ache in his gut was getting worse. He needed to get out of here. But so did Viktor.

Viktor shook his head. "She's dead if we cut her loose."

Sasha didn't give a damn about the woman. Viktor, on the other hand... "You need to watch your back."

The friend, Jake, stiffened. "Are you threatening him?"

Sweat beaded on his brow and the wound in his side flashed hot. They needed to leave. Now.

"Stand down, Jake," Viktor interjected. "It isn't what it seems."

"We need to get her to ALIAS before she wakes up." Jake still held the unconscious woman.

And Sasha needed Viktor to walk away. He looked at Viktor. He wasn't sure he'd ever see him again. That reality stabbed at him—as painful as the knife wound in his side. He wanted to hug him, kiss him one last time, but witnesses made that impossible. He could no longer picture a future where they were together. It had been a silly dream anyway. "Take care of yourself, *dorogoy*. It's time to leave."

Sasha swayed again. Dammit, his side hurt.

Viktor grabbed his arm. "Wait. What is wrong with you?"

Everything. Nothing.

Sasha tried to pull his arm away. "You need to get her out of here. If we found her, then whoever paid her is bound to find her too."

"You're right." Viktor's fingers caressed Sasha's leather sleeve. "Jake. Can you handle her?"

"Uh, sure." Jake glanced at him. "Vik, can I talk to you a minute? Alone?"

Viktor ran his gaze over Sasha. "How did you get here?"

"Public transportation." Perhaps attempting to take the Metro had been a poor choice after the last time.

Viktor tossed him a set of keys. "Get in my truck. I'll be there in a second."

"Are you sure that's wise?" Jake said.

"Wise? No. It's not." Viktor began to wipe down the hotel room. "But I need answers."

Jake wasn't wrong. Sasha shouldn't get in Viktor's truck.

Viktor bulleted out commands. "Scan the parking lot, make sure we don't have company yet."

"*You're* giving *me* orders?" A smile tugged at Sasha's lips, his heart warming.

"Damn straight."

"Vik, maybe you should just come with me." Jake was still trying to separate them.

"You are trying to protect him." Sasha nodded. "Good. This is good. Get him out of here."

"What the hell is going on?" Viktor reached for Sasha.

He needed to sit down soon. His knees dipped and Viktor caught him.

"Shit. You're bleeding."

Sasha looked down. The stain on his shirt was spreading. "Huh."

His head swirled again.

Viktor's face went sheet white. He tugged Sasha to the worn, polyester bedspread. "Sit. Before you fall down."

"Russians lower to the ground gracefully. We don't fall," he said arrogantly. But he ruined that proclamation with a deep groan. *Gav-no*, it hurt.

"Shut up." Viktor commanded Sasha, then turned to Jake. "Get her to ALIAS, please."

"What about you and"—Jake gave a chin lift—"him?"

"I'll take care of him. Then we will wait for the asshole who set us up." Viktor frowned.

"But—"

Viktor shooed Jake toward the door. "This guy has already killed two people. Let's not add to his tally."

* * *

*S*asha was hurt. Viktor should still be angry but seeing him in pain had wiped away his initial anger. What he wanted to do was wrap him in a hug and hold on tight. "How bad?"

"I'll live."

So it was bad. Viktor tossed Sasha a towel. "Press this against your side while I help get her in the car."

"I'll take care of her." Jake stared hard at Viktor but didn't ask the questions burning in his gaze. He hoisted the woman in his arms and headed for his sedan.

Viktor opened the back door and strapped the woman in. Then he zip-tied her hands together.

Jake stared at the woman's bound wrists, his expression tortured. "Do we have to do that?"

"Just until you get her to the safe room at ALIAS," Viktor cautioned. "I don't want her to cause an accident if she wakes up while you're driving."

Jake nodded. "Good point. I've got her." He glanced back at the motel room. "You sure you know what you're doing?"

"No." Viktor's heart bumped erratically. He had no fucking clue what he was doing. "But I can't let him go yet."

He was afraid if he did, he'd never see Sasha again. There'd been regret in his gaze, and a finality in Sasha's voice that wiped away the anger Viktor had been nursing and left him empty. Sasha had filled a hole in Viktor that had been there for a long time. He itched to get back to Sasha, to tend to him, to find out what had happened. His black eye had yellowed some, but he still looked beat up.

Jake frowned. "If you need anything, I got your back."

Viktor said, "Thank you. I owe you."

"We're friends. That's what friends do." Jake glanced inside the car. "I'd better get going. Does Jill know we're coming?"

"I'll text her."

Jake got in his battered old Jeep and drove away. Viktor grabbed sterile wipes from the medical kit he always carried with him, and then headed back inside to interrogate his former lover.

This room with its dirty shag carpeting and worn, faded polyester bedspread was a perfect metaphor of their relationship. He wanted fine cotton sheets and luxurious bathrobes, but he deserved a filthy, ancient slum.

Sasha hadn't moved from the bed. He sat hunched over, one arm across his middle.

"Take off your shirt." Viktor's heart thundered, banging against his ribs as Sasha unbuttoned his shirt. "What happened?"

"Stabbed," Sasha grunted.

Viktor swallowed the bile that rose as he spread open the bloodstained shirt.

Sasha studied him with a bewildered look on his face. "You get queasy at the sight of blood."

"Yes." He'd admitted to that before.

"Then why did you become a medic?"

"Because they asked me to." And because he wasn't crazy about killing either. Being a medic was a way to serve his adopted country and save people rather than kill them. However, he was very happy when he transferred to the CIA after he got his degree in military history.

"I do not understand you." Sasha shook his head. "All these choices and yet you agree to do something that makes you sick."

"I am grateful for my country." Viktor sweated through cleaning the wound.

"What has your country done for you?"

"This is not Russia."

"We have no time for this," Sasha argued.

"Where were you stabbed?"

"In the torso." Sasha gestured to his side. "You see this."

Viktor growled. "You misunderstand on purpose."

"Fine. In the Metro station."

"Another attack in the Metro?"

"Da."

"Maybe find a new method of transportation."

Sasha laughed, then groaned, bending slightly at the waist. "Da."

"This isn't funny. You could have been killed." Viktor used sterile wipes to clean Sasha's flesh with gentle, trembling fingers.

"We need to hurry." Sasha rolled his hand in a get moving motion. "Whoever is after the woman may be here soon."

"And they may take hours." Viktor gathered all the trash from cleaning the wound. "We will stakeout the room from my truck, and I will sew up the wound there."

"Leave the room as is," Sasha countered. "Let them think there's been a fight."

There had been. Viktor took one last look around the hotel room, making sure that they hadn't left anything that could tie back to them.

Sasha curled his arm around Viktor and let him help him to the truck. Once they were settled, Viktor got down to the business of sewing up Sasha's wound.

He pulled the curved needle and suture thread from his kit. He sterilized the area as best he could, then used the tissue forceps to manipulate Sasha's skin. Wielding the needle driver, he inserted the needle at a ninety-degree angle. He took a deep breath to center himself.

"Just slap a bandage on it."

"No." Viktor began sewing the flesh together in a continuous suturing technique. He tried not to think about the fact that he was sewing together Sasha's skin. "I am sorry I don't have any anesthesia."

"It is of no consequence." Sasha stared out the window. "Just get it done."

"My FSB guy. So tough." Viktor sewed quickly, needing to get this over with. He tied off the suture thread and tossed the forceps, needle driver, and needle back in his medical kit. He kissed his lover's shoulder, his skin smooth and hot beneath his lips. "Heal fast."

"Is this an American remedy?" Amusement layered his voice.

"If you like."

"You kiss all your patients?" he growled.

Viktor thought about tossing off a flippant answer. After all, Sasha had told him the only reason he had sex with him was because it was a pleasurable way to extract information. "Only the ones who use me first."

Sasha grabbed Viktor's head and slammed his mouth against his. The kiss was short, brutal, and over too soon.

"I like my remedy better." Sasha grinned.

Viktor did too. More than he should.

He handed Sasha some Tylenol. He dry swallowed the pills while Viktor stowed his medical kit in the backseat.

They settled in the front seat of Viktor's truck. He'd parked at the edge of the crumbling pavement. Garbage and twigs and snow snuggled the edges, pushed aside by a plow, the forgotten detritus lived on the edge of civilization like the inhabitants of the no-tell motel. The angle of the truck camouflaged his license plate from the rest of the parking lot. He'd chosen the shadows, with only one working overhead streetlamp near the motel office; the rest of the lights were broken and the parking lot cloaked in darkness.

Viktor had grabbed a pillow and rested it against the backseat trying to cushion Sasha.

"You should drink some water." He wanted to hover like a mother hen.

"Not yet." Sasha shook his head. "I don't want to have to urinate in a bottle."

The atmosphere in the confines of the truck was intimate and close.

They sat in a silence that held questions and secrets. Viktor hated to break their tentative bubble of companionship, but it was time to get some answers. Especially since Sasha had information on who had killed the bartender.

"So, you know who killed Mack?"

"Da."

"Are you going to share?" he asked with exasperation.

Sasha hesitated.

A car drove by the muffler rumbling and growling. They waited to see if the vehicle turned in the parking lot, but the car continued on.

Another car, sleeker and quieter, followed. They watched as that car also drove by.

"My employers," Sasha finally admitted.

Viktor jerked. His employers had set up the bartender and paid him? But Viktor had been recruited by the Cigarette Man. "You tracked the payment?"

"I'd rather not say how I know."

"You're sure they didn't pay the women?"

"I could find no evidence that they hired the *prostitutkas*."

"But they were clearly working for the same purpose. Get kompromat. The women were back-up if Mack failed."

"Perhaps it was a joint operation," Sasha postured. "They just kept the two cells separate."

"Cells?" Viktor rolled his eyes. "These were not trained operatives. They used amateurs luring them with money."

"Easier to get rid of without much oversight," Sasha said.

He wasn't wrong. And if they got caught, as the woman had been, her information was relatively worthless.

They continued to wait. They couldn't keep the car on—that would draw attention to them—and the air outside was frigid. The temperature fell with each passing minute. Mist lingered with the puff of their breath.

Viktor pulled an emergency blanket from the backseat and draped it over them.

"Boy Scout," Sasha taunted, but it lacked heat.

Viktor snorted. "Boy Scouts are for families and happy fathers and sons."

"Your family was not happy?"

Viktor's father had been completely demoralized by every uphill battle he'd faced after defecting. "The American dream is not for everyone. That's just what they want you to think."

"I thought you liked America."

"I do. But my father had expectations that did not come true. He was…unhappy."

An understatement of epic proportions. His father had been angry all the time. He'd taken out his frustration and rage on him and his mother. As if they'd had any say in defecting.

"You said before, defecting wasn't what he expected." There was a flatness in Sasha's voice, but Viktor was lost in his childhood memories.

"When my father's hopes did not come to pass, he turned to a favorite Russian pastime. Drowning his unhappiness in cheap vodka." Much like he would have done if he had stayed in Russia.

"Ah." Now Sasha would understand the reason for Viktor's hatred of vodka.

"My father's American experience has been one long disappointment." Viktor pushed back against the headrest, staring at a small hole in the cloth ceiling of his truck. "It only got worse as I got older, and it was apparent that I did not share his big strapping Russian manly gene. I preferred books and quiet and learning to more physical pursuits. But he was proud of me when I went into the military. I was never sure if it was because I was shooting guns, which I hated, or because then I couldn't admit that I was gay."

* * *

Sasha's heart ached for young Viktor.

His father's disappointments had clearly affected him very much.

"I never knew my papa." Sasha was melancholy. His mother had been a widow by the time he'd been born. She told him tales of his father's bravery and service to Russia. But as an adult he could look back and wonder if she'd only told him those stories to make him proud.

"Did your mother know…."

"That I am *gey*."

"Yes."

"We never spoke of it. But she stopped asking me when I was going to get married and give her chubby Russian babies, so I believe she did." It was her compromise. Plus he'd never actually said the words out loud to her, to *anyone*, until now.

"I am attracted to men." His heart thumped in his chest and his palms were slick with sweat that had nothing to do with his knife wound.

"I know."

"I've…never admitted this aloud."

"Never?"

"Nyet."

"My *dorogoy*." Viktor reached out and squeezed Sasha's knee. "Look! The world did not end."

"It would if the wrong people heard me." Sasha rubbed his hand over his heart. Yet did it matter?

Viktor's smile disappeared. "I know." He ran his palm over the knit cap on Sasha's head. The caress sweet, affectionate.

"I am attracted to *you*." There. Sasha had said it. He shouldn't have. He should have left well enough alone and not complicated this already insanely complex situation.

Viktor grabbed his hand and then leaned in to kiss him.

His lips were soft and firm against Sasha's. The kiss was one of tenderness. Of affection. So unlike his previous interactions with men.

The interior of the truck reminded him too much of his other furtive encounters. He'd had an unexpected period of respite with Viktor in his apartment. A moment out of time, his reward for a life about to be cut short.

Sasha cupped Viktor's jaw. "I am grateful for this time we had."

"Why does this sound like goodbye?"

Because he would be gone soon. But he couldn't tell Viktor, for his own safety. "If we were other people, if we came from a different time and place, then maybe…"

"I don't like the implications of this talk," Viktor said.

Sasha spun out his fantasy. "I can imagine a simple cottage in a rural town by the sea." He'd wander about with his camera, shooting photographs and perhaps fishing for dinner. Enjoying the peace of a bucolic homestead.

"I could read by the fire," Viktor said.

And clean his weapons, Sasha thought. But maybe in this dream life, Viktor wouldn't need weapons. "After an intimate dinner, we could do the dishes together."

"You wash. I dry." Viktor smiled.

"Then we could have sex on the hooked rug by the fire."

"And retire with a glass of cognac to our four-poster bed under the eaves." Viktor had a faraway look in his eyes.

It was an enjoyable fantasy. But they were not meant to be.

"It's not impossible," Viktor argued, even though Sasha hadn't said a word.

He couldn't let Viktor think this could ever come to pass. "It is impossible."

"Is this why you pushed me away?"

"I was trying to protect you."

"I am a big boy." Viktor shifted to face him. "Capable of taking care of myself."

"There is too much danger around me. Too many people wanting to hurt me." Sasha couldn't bear it if something happened to Viktor. "I would be devastated if you were hurt, or worse."

Viktor hesitated. "There is something I need to tell you."

An American model car, from the eighties, beat up and dented, indeterminate color, pulled into the parking lot. It was the kind of car people avoided looking at. No one wanted to imagine a reality so depressing.

Sasha tensed. Perhaps this is who they had been waiting for.

"I need—"

"Shh. Let's see if this is our guy. You can tell me later." Sasha pulled out a digital camera from the small backpack. "Hopefully it didn't get damaged during the altercation."

"But it's important—"

Viktor stopped mid-sentence as the man exited the car. He had parked right under the only working lamp in the parking lot. Sasha took in details cataloguing the man and his appearance as he snapped pictures. He looked like he was homeless. Dreadlocks and baggy dirty clothing and...dress shoes? Sasha zoomed in on the man's very scruffy hidden face and then, because the shoes were an anomaly, he focused in on those.

Viktor's mouth slammed shut. "Shit."

"You know him?"

Viktor swallowed, his Adam's apple bobbing. "He's the something I need to tell you about." The fear on Viktor's face and in his eyes triggered a klaxon alarm in Sasha's head.

What?

This was going to be bad.

Chapter 15

*V*iktor had to tell Sasha about Cigarette Man.

He was here. At the motel room, where they had found the woman. He'd promised that he hadn't killed the bartender. He hadn't ever confirmed that he had hired Mack and now Sasha had evidence that the FSB hired Mack, but not the women. Mack drugged them and left them to the two women.

Had Cigarette Man hired the women? Sasha's intelligence indicated the woman and Mack had been killed by Russian assassins.

That had to mean the Russians and Cigarette Man were working together. Right?

As soon as Cigarette Man went into the motel room, by tacit agreement, they slid down in the seat so they weren't visible.

"I need to tell you now." His stomach pitched and rolled. A peculiar fear shivered through him. Because he knew that Sasha was going to feel betrayed.

Sasha watched the doorway to the hotel room.

"I wasn't in the bar randomly." Viktor blurted out.

"You told me this."

"But I didn't tell you that I was there because I was doing reconnaissance. I was being blackmailed into into getting kompromat on you." Viktor wanted to throw up.

Sasha's head whipped around. Like prey that sensed a predator, Sasha held hyper-still. He said nothing, waiting for Viktor to finish.

The silence expanded inside the truck, like a physical presence that threatened to overwhelm Viktor. He could barely hear over the beating of his heart.

Sasha pivoted to watch the doorway so his face was hidden. "Why wait tell me until now?" His voice was toneless.

"Because at first it didn't seem relevant. He hadn't really gotten anything that could be used against you." In fact, all the fall out of that night pointed toward problems for Viktor. That stray thought whispered through his brain.

He wanted to embrace Sasha, but his body language was closed off and the tension in his frame told Viktor everything.

"When I agreed…I didn't know you. You were just a guy in a photo," Viktor said desperately. "I just knew that my fuck-up had put my friends in danger and that I'd been presented with an opportunity to fix it."

"So having sex with me was a job." Sasha laughed but it was an ugly sound.

"No!" Desperation clawed at Viktor. "You have to know that isn't true."

"Ironic. That's one avenue I never used while pursuing my targets." Despite the fact that he'd indicated that earlier.

Viktor could feel Sasha slipping away. He wondered if he'd ever really had him. Maybe their whole relationship had been an illusion.

"I didn't have sex with you because of that."

"So you say." Sasha shrugged as if the past few weeks

didn't matter. As if what was between them was nothing. Less than nothing. "What is the man's name?"

"I don't know."

Sasha shot him a disgusted look. "Who does he work for?"

"I don't know."

"How could you agree to spy for a man you know nothing about?"

"My boss vouched for him," Viktor replied.

"Did you do any investigating?"

No. He'd taken Jill's word for it. Except she'd been trying to find out more details since people started turning up dead. She hadn't really trusted the man either.

"You know that your superior does not have your interests at heart."

"You don't understand," Viktor said. "She wouldn't betray me."

"So you say."

"These are my friends. Not my enemies."

Sasha snorted. "There are no friends."

"What an incredible lonely way to live."

"Never mind." Sasha shook his head. "It doesn't matter."

They watched as the man stormed out of the hotel room. He glanced around the parking lot, his gaze skimming over their truck.

Viktor held still, waiting.

The man bent down to peer underneath and circled his car. Finally, after more time than he'd spent in the hotel room, he got in and slammed shut the door. He started his car, the engine roaring to life with a growl, belying the beater look.

"We follow. Da?"

"Yes."

They waited until Cigarette Man pulled out of the parking

lot and then, staying far behind, tailed him. "I wish we'd had time to put a tracker on the car," Viktor said.

"He is a professional." He had checked for bombs, even though he'd only been in the motel room for a few minutes.

Viktor commented, "He told us he didn't kill the bartender."

"He didn't," Sasha said.

"And you recognized the MO on the sex worker's death as one of your people." Viktor talked through what was bothering him.

"Da."

"But he clearly wasn't here to help the woman."

He'd always known this man wasn't his friend. But now, he was the enemy.

"Nyet."

Sasha's responses were short. A heavy weight pressed down on him like a black cloud. He'd betrayed Sasha's trust. He wanted it back, desperately. But right now, they had to figure out what was going on with Cigarette Man.

They followed him. Viktor's brain worked at hyper speed. Everything was pointing to more than one player. Cigarette Man may not have killed Mack or the woman but he knew people were dying. There was no way that the US government had sanctioned that. Was the guy working for someone else? Was he working on his own? What was happening?

The safety of the other sex worker was priority. She could identify the man who'd hired her, who was now linked to two homicides.

Cigarette Man was taking a long, meandering surveillance detection route. Viktor turned off. "We cannot follow him any longer. We do not want to be spotted." The snow had begun to fall in sheets and the roads were nearly deserted at this time of night. "We will be noticed if we continue."

"Agree." Sasha pounded his fist on the dash. "We are at a standstill."

"The woman is at ALIAS with Jake. As long as she stays there, she will be protected. We can show her a picture of him and find out if he's the one who hired her and the dead woman."

"Let's call it for this evening," Sasha said. "Drop me off near my apartment."

Viktor grunted. There was no way he was leaving Sasha alone right now.

Sasha yawned, his mouth opened so wide, his jaw cracked.

"I am going to run an extended SDR to make sure he doesn't somehow double back and follow us. Rest." Viktor commanded.

Sasha nodded and let his eyes drift closed.

Then Viktor did what he had to do.

* * *

*S*asha woke to silence. And darkness.

He regained consciousness slowly, unlike his regular waking routine, his head fuzzy and an ache in his side, his body stiff with lingering pain.

He'd been stabbed.

And had killed another assassin sent to eliminate him. He needed to stay off the grid until he could get a handle on what was going on, put all his ducks in a row (a stupid American saying that he found himself saying anyway). If he was going down, he was taking as many people with him as he could.

He kept his eyes closed, assessing his surroundings, testing the atmosphere.

The scent of air freshener underlain with the odor of French fries.

The last thing he remembered was falling asleep in Viktor's truck. Viktor who had betrayed him. He realized he was still in the truck, but they were no longer moving. However, he sensed no danger.

He opened his eyes slowly.

They were in some sort of underground garage. Sasha glanced through the windshield and took in details. It wasn't very big, and didn't appear familiar, so Viktor's apartment building was out.

Where the fuck had Viktor brought him?

In the driver's seat, Viktor stretched. "You're awake." His voice was gravelly with sleep.

He was trying to stay mad at him. Viktor had set him up. He should have known that Viktor had been put in his path to tempt him. Now, when he was almost free.

"Where are we?"

"Adams-Larsen."

What? "You brought me to your employer?" Was this more betrayal? He couldn't seem to clarify his thoughts. It was as if he were wading through a fog of regret unable to see the truth. More than anger, he was just…sad.

"We need answers about Cigarette Man. And we need to see if the woman can identify him as the person who hired her."

"Cigarette Man?"

"That's what I call him." Viktor slumped against the driver's door. "I'm—"

He interrupted. He didn't want to hear excuses. "Why would you bring *me* here?" He kept trying to protect Viktor, whether he deserved it or not, and instead Viktor kept doing things to endanger himself.

"To help you."

"I don't need help," Sasha said arrogantly.

"Does that tone work with people?"

"Da. They are afraid of me." As they should be.

"Sorry to disappoint," Viktor said, but there was a tinge of laughter in his voice.

"I cannot be here." Sasha had a desperate need to get away before someone discovered him and put Viktor in danger.

"Relax. This is an underground garage. We only use it for very special clients. The entrance to the interior of the building is not visible anywhere. The only person who can see us is whoever is on guard duty in the security room." Viktor stretched his arms above his head, the Henley shirt he wore pulling up and exposing his flat, rippled abs. "Let's go get more comfortable."

Sasha hesitated.

"Don't worry." Viktor patted his shoulder. "I've got you covered."

They headed into the secure building. Motion sensor lights lit up along the corridor after Viktor used a palm reader and alphanumeric keypad to gain access. Sasha followed with trepidation.

They walked past a viewing window showing a padded sparring room with racks of weights along one wall, fitness machines in the corner, a row of hooks with some sort of puffy suit along another wall, and a large mat in the middle of the room.

Sasha took in the lighting, the cameras, the security. This was not a casual operation.

Viktor led him to a small break room with a refrigerator, a row of cabinets and an industrial table in the corner. A Keurig sat on the counter. "You want a coffee? Tea?"

The man, Jake, from the hotel room burst into the room. "What is he doing here?"

Exactly what Sasha thought.

"We need to talk to the woman," Viktor replied calmly.

"Dude. WTF?"

Sasha nodded.

"He shouldn't be here."

Sasha nodded again and Viktor shot him a dark look. "We came in the underground entrance."

"Have you seen the news?" Jake said. "His picture is all over it. He pushed a guy in the Metro station onto the tracks and killed him."

"He was stabbed before he pushed in self-defense," Viktor shot back.

Kill or be killed. But his timetable had moved up again. Sasha sighed. "Let's talk to her then I will go."

"No!"

"Then you go?" Jake said.

"Yes." Then he would leave.

* * *

A few hours later, Sasha and Viktor were in the safe room where the woman had been kept. Somehow he still hadn't left.

The room held a queen-sized bed, a sitting area with two chairs and a television, and a small counter in the corner with a mini-fridge underneath and coffee maker. A compact bathroom with a shower stall and toilet completed the set up.

The slight scent of vomit lingered in the air. Mr. Hardass, Jake, had thrown up after the woman had been terrified and they'd had to give her a sedative to calm her down.

She had identified Cigarette Man as the person who had hired her. He had used the prostitutes to compromise clients. Jillian Larsen, Viktor's boss, had been called in and they were dealing with getting the woman into protective custody.

Sasha needed to go, but first he needed more information from Viktor. "You need to tell me everything," he demanded.

"A few months ago, I screwed up and slept with the wrong man," Viktor confessed. "That exposed our agency to public scrutiny."

"What does Adams-Larsen really do?" Sasha had asked before, but Viktor had been cagey. The fact that this Cigarette Man had tried to blackmail Viktor meant something else was at play here. He needed all the information so that he could protect Viktor.

"I can't tell you." Viktor looked contrite but Sasha needed answers. "I can't betray my boss's confidence. We are in this situation because of my screw up."

Damn him and his honor.

"Tell me what the man wanted. Exactly," Sasha demanded.

Viktor led him through the initial conversation.

"I think he is trying to compromise *you*."

"Me?" Viktor shifted in his seat. "To what end?"

Sasha tapped a finger against his lips as he ran through various scenarios. "I do not believe this was ever about me."

"But it is now?"

"We were put in each other's paths for a reason. By two separate entities," Sasha said.

"Why me?" Viktor seemed bewildered. "I work for an image consulting firm."

"You were placed in front of me as a potential double agent."

Viktor snorted. "Where would I get intel? And who would I give it to?"

"Exactly." That was what Sasha had told Dubov. And yet he had insisted that Sasha follow Viktor. Things were off.

"They don't understand me at all," Viktor marveled.

"I would guess they believe your estrangement from your parents is incentive to spy for Russia."

Viktor blinked. "Really?"

Sasha nodded slowly, watching Viktor closely. Viktor laughed, deep from his belly. He bent over his stomach contracting and rippling with the force of his laughter. Tears pooled in the corners of his eyes, sparkling with amusement.

"So you have no interested in spying?"

"Not at all." Viktor skimmed his fingers over Sasha's with a light caress. "I have enough secrets to worry about these days."

Sasha smiled, but it was tinged with sadness. That was all they could ever be...a secret.

Sasha didn't think Viktor understood the gravity of what was happening here. He turned serious. "You need to take precautions. They are setting you up."

"I think you're wrong. I can't be compromised."

Sasha's frustration grew. He had to make Viktor understand. "They pushed us together. They dangled you as a source. They told me to investigate you as a potential double agent and spy for America. I think they wanted us to," he gestured between them. "so they could blackmail you to work for them."

And...

"Not going to happen." Viktor pressed, "What is the *and* part of that sentence?"

"How do you mean?"

"Blackmail me and...what? They didn't have just one objective, did they?"

"They want me dead."

"What?" Viktor shoved to attention.

"They were going to ask me to kill the traitor."

Viktor's green eyes widened. "Should you be telling me

this? I don't think I should know this. If they find out you shared, you could be in trouble."

"You need to know…when something happens to me, don't pursue it."

Viktor shoved out of his chair and began to pace. "What in God's name have you done?"

"Too much to go into here." Sasha was confused as to why Viktor was so upset. "I have money…I'd like you to have it."

"Why are you talking like you're going to be dead?"

"Because I am," he said matter-of-factly. "They are already trying to kill me, and they have no idea of half of what I've done."

"You believe you're going to die."

"Da." He had to die. "But I will confess that I didn't realize how much it would hurt to say goodbye to you."

"I don't want to say goodbye." Viktor clutched at Sasha's shoulders.

"You have made my final weeks bearable." Sasha brushed his palm over Viktor's neck, then cupped his jaw. He pressed a tender kiss to his lips. "I am sorry to leave you."

"Stop," Viktor said. "This is crazy. Why would they kill you?"

"They have already tried. Multiple times. They must understand that I no longer support Russia and the things we have done. Putin and the FSB will see this as the ultimate betrayal. And they do not tolerate betrayal."

Not just this, but everything that Sasha had done. When he'd started on this path, he hadn't factored a lover into his equation.

It wouldn't have mattered. He needed to leave Russia. He needed to leave this life that no longer fit him. He needed to atone for his actions. He was ready.

Sasha had wanted them to pay. Of course, he'd wanted to

live. But he'd figured that if his life was forfeit, then so be it. He hadn't anticipated meeting Viktor. He hadn't anticipated meeting *anyone*. He'd never even given himself permission to hope for a relationship.

"How does sleeping with me translate to a betrayal?"

Sometimes Viktor was so American. "I have been working with the American government. I have given them much information about the various 'accidents' here."

"You're the man that you're supposed to be looking for." Shock colored his voice. Viktor had finally figured it out. *Sasha* was the traitor.

* * *

*V*iktor was trying to process everything.

Sasha was working with the United States. But that meant... "How many people know you're a spy?"

Sasha shrugged. "They know I exist, but I don't know how many people know my identity."

"You had to know this was a death sentence." Viktor struggled to figure out all the nuances of this situation.

Either the Cigarette Man didn't know Sasha was the one giving intelligence to the US government and he hoped he could blackmail Sasha into telling them who was, or he did know and he was somehow...setting Sasha up? Or maybe he was trying to recruit Sasha just like he'd said in their initial meeting.

"I knew it was a possibility."

A bubbling, burning anger fueled Viktor's fury. "And what...you didn't think your life was worth anything?"

"That is not exactly how I saw it." Sasha shrugged. "I was angry. Disenfranchised."

"You must have examined the consequences."

"Of course. I plan for every possibility when undertaking any mission."

"But not this." Viktor wagged his finger between the two of them.

"Finding you was never even a blip on my radar. I never expected…" He trailed off.

Viktor's rage cooled, because Sasha looked bewildered.

"How can you plan for something that you've never even hoped for?" Sasha shrugged, his palms in the air. "Love, for someone like me, is too dangerous. Too forbidden."

Viktor froze.

Love.

"I never saw you coming." Sasha wrapped his arms around Viktor in a melancholy embrace and squeezed. "At the time I began this journey, I didn't know that the life I would have was worth living."

Viktor's heart broke.

"Trust is hard," Sasha confessed.

Viktor had feelings for this man. Great big messy feelings. He swallowed past the lump in his throat. "I don't want you to die."

"Not fond of the idea myself."

Jake knocked on the door. "Vik."

He had to go. He had to get the woman to the US Marshals. They had gotten a temporary order to protect her until her evidence could be vetted and the proper authorities notified.

"Stay. Sleep," Viktor begged. "We can figure this out when I return."

But when he returned, Sasha was gone.

Chapter 16

Sasha waited until he was sure Viktor had left. Then he ventured out from the small windowless apartment, located inside the old brownstone. Another suspicious detail. Why would an image consulting firm need a safe room?

A voice came over the speaker. "Dinna exit the room."

Well that answered that question. The safe room had cameras. But Viktor hadn't locked the door. So he wasn't a prisoner. Very confusing.

A slender man with dark rumpled hair came running down the hall at him.

Sasha held his arms out at his sides, attempting to show he was unarmed. The man pulled up and stared at him, indecision written all over his face. "Are you daft? What are you doing?"

"I would like to speak with Jillian Larsen."

"I need to search ya for weapons." The man's Scottish accent was thick with suspicion.

"I have nothing dangerous with me." Truth. He could be dangerous. However, Sasha meant them no harm.

The man scoffed. "Arms out at your sides."

He expertly searched Sasha from his neck down to his shoes. He decided not to mention that he didn't need a weapon to kill the man. But as the Scot assessed him, he thought perhaps this man already knew that.

Sasha suffered through the pat-down. He understood the caution. But it still annoyed him. He didn't have time to waste. He needed to be gone before Viktor returned. "Jillian Larsen?"

"You're lucky you're still here. I was firmly against it."

He didn't like feeling quite so exposed even though they were near no windows or doors. "Jillian Larsen?"

"If you touch her…if you so much as twitch at her…I will end you. And hide your body."

"Hamish." The disembodied voice of a woman, full of exasperation, flooded the hallway. "Please show our guest to my office."

Sasha had done research on the "image consulting" agency but he didn't have any intelligence on an employee named Hamish.

A white woman, blonde, Nordic, with gray eyes and a pencil skirt, greeted him just inside the doorway to her office. "Sasha, I'm Jillian Larsen." She held out her hand to shake.

Clearly Jillian Larsen didn't have the same reservations as her Scottish guard dog.

"Sasha Loblaw." The Scot followed behind, crowding close to Sasha, like a pesky terrier. "Can we speak privately?"

"Do you promise not to hurt me?"

"Da."

She studied him one more time. "What is your intent in coming here?"

"I would have stayed away, but Viktor brought me when I was asleep." He decided to be brutally honest. "Otherwise, we would never have met."

"You fell asleep in his truck?"

"Da."

"You must trust him immeasurably."

"I do." A sense of amazement shuddered through him. He hadn't trusted anyone since he was a young boy. But he trusted Viktor. And he was going to make sure Viktor was protected. "I need to talk to you about Viktor."

She inclined her head regally. "Hamish, can you man the security booth?"

"I really don't like this," Hamish practically growled.

"Duly noted." Jillian placed her fingertips on the man's forearm. "But I believe Mr. Loblaw needs privacy to discuss his concerns."

Sasha watched the interaction between the two. There was something more than employer/employee there.

"I'll be okay." Jillian Larsen smiled. The Scot was having none of it and he shot Sasha a dark look before he left.

"Have a seat." She gestured to a chair across from the massive desk. Then she took a seat behind the desk where Sasha guessed she had easy access to a weapon. Smart and beautiful.

She had a quality of command, she clearly ruled the office, but she seemed to rule with compassion, rather than fear. Sasha understood why she appealed to Viktor.

"You are the boss lady, da?"

She kept a polite smile on her face.

"You will look out for him?"

The ice queen frowned, her brow crinkling. "Of course."

That was not what she was expecting. He liked to do the unexpected. It amused him to watch people scramble to keep up. But this was too important to play games.

"He will continue to pursue this dangerous investigation if we do not stop him."

"Agree. He's been through too much." Jillian drummed her fingers on her desktop. "I don't want him hurt."

They were in agreement there.

"You don't intend to hurt him, do you?" she asked.

Sasha rubbed at his chest over his heart, yearning for something he couldn't have, wishing that his life could turn out differently. That he and Viktor could have a chance to be together for more than a few nights. A chance at a normal life.

But what was normal? Sasha didn't know. He did know that he ached with the loss of that possibility. It was too late for him. Hopefully Viktor would one day find a partner. Was it wrong that he wanted to kill that unknown, faceless partner? For taking what he wanted, for stealing away the life he could never have?

"Are you going to hurt him?" she repeated.

Probably. But not on purpose.

"He was right," Sasha murmured, a sort of wonder filling him. Viktor's boss *did* care for him.

"About what?"

"You will look out for him."

"Of course." She answered as if there was never any question.

That kind of support was unheard of in the FSB or the Kremlin. "That is not the way of my employer."

Jillian Larsen held his gaze, her gray eyes stormy with emotion. "I'm more than his employer. I'm his friend."

"And friends watch out for each other." This too was a foreign concept for him. But he was glad that Viktor would have this woman to champion him. "I need to share with you. I believe your integrity is solid."

She straightened in her seat, her shoulders back and a frown on her face.

"I believe someone is targeting Viktor. This is why I ask for your assurance that you will look out for him."

"What do you mean?"

"He was dangled in front of me as a possible spy. I was directed to investigate him."

"A Russian spy?" She made a chopping motion with her hand. "That's ridiculous."

Sasha dipped his chin. "After spending time with him, he is not remotely who my superiors wanted me to believe."

"What makes you think he's a target?"

"There are no coincidences," Sasha said. "They tell me to look into him. Throw us together. Drug us. And now someone, more than just my employer, is cleaning up loose ends. The bartender. The woman."

"That is...not good." She seemed to be considering his information.

"Nyet." His stomach sloshed at the thought of Viktor being coerced. He needed to come up with a plan to stop them.

"What do you suggest?"

"At the moment, I do not know." But he would have to figure it out. Soon. He needed to die. "But your job is only to protect Viktor."

"Okay," she said slowly.

"We have an understanding?"

She sat at the desk, composed, but he sensed a seething concern beneath her calm face. "I absolutely promise to look out for Viktor."

"Okay, now that is settled." Sasha took a deep breath. "You help people disappear."

Jill studied him.

"Do not worry. I am not looking for anyone that you helped."

"We didn't help Sergei Polzin disappear," she offered.

He believed her. He had seen a picture of the dead body. Not that death couldn't be faked. But the bullet holes in Polzin were hard to ignore. Polzin was most definitely dead.

Sasha noted that she very carefully did not answer his question.

"You don't help people die."

"We do not."

"No explosions, accidental drownings, car bombings, lost at sea…fake deaths?"

"Sorry. Fake deaths are not in our wheelhouse."

But she had worked for the US Marshals. He knew this because of his investigation of Adams-Larsen. He hadn't liked how committed Viktor was to his employer. He was trying to tie up loose ends. He had wanted to assess whether these people had Viktor's best interests at heart. Though the circumstances behind her exit from the government agency were not public knowledge, Sasha had sources.

There was something fishy about her last assignment with the marshals and the death of their witness. To Sasha it seemed as if perhaps the witness was not actually dead.

Although the business of faking deaths was not something he had much experience with, there had been targets on occasion that had tried. However, the FSB had always found them and made them pay. But Sasha could still hope.

"It is too bad you are not in the business of faking deaths."

"We're strictly a public image consultant firm."

"I know this is not true." Sasha leaned toward her.

An intercom went on. "Back away from the desk."

"I am not going to hurt her." Sasha rolled his eyes.

She tapped the desk blotter with a pen, waiting for him to continue.

"You cannot help me with my image."

"I am sorry. But I cannot," Jillian replied.

"The rumblings I hear is that you help people disappear."

"The rumblings I hear is that you kill people," she snapped back.

Sasha raised his eyebrows. "You have teeth. That is good."

"Is it true?"

"It was. Not all that I do. However, I do not want to do that anymore." Sasha was tired. Tired of the violence, tired of the death, tired of the lack of control. "But my employer is not one who allows me to quit."

"I *am* sorry," she said it softly. As if she were considering.

"I have no need of a new identity." He already had his exit plan in place. Sasha had known talking with her and hoping she could help solve his problems was a long shot. "Take care of him when I am gone."

"You're leaving?"

"I will be dead soon."

Jillian Larsen stood. "You really believe that is the only way to break free? Death?"

"Da." Otherwise they would never let him go. "I don't want him to mourn me. Please watch over him."

He'd set out what he needed to do. And he'd been in this place for far too long.

"It is time for me to go." Sasha glanced around the office, the last time he'd have any contact that meant anything to Viktor. "Thank you for looking out for him."

"You...care about him." Jillian leaned back in her chair, looking confused. Surprised, maybe? He couldn't decipher the look on her face.

"I will die for him." Because if he didn't, Viktor might pay the price.

"Hamish, can you come in here?" She bit her lip. "I may have a solution."

* * *

He'd been devastated when he got back to ALIAS and Sasha was gone. He had tried for hours to reach Sasha, even went to his apartments, both decoy and real, but it was as if he'd disappeared.

As soon as work was over, he planned to head to Sasha's secret apartment. But an uncomfortable edginess tickled at the back of his mind.

Maybe Sasha hadn't forgiven him for not telling him about Cigarette Man earlier. But he could make it up to him. He knew they could figure it out together. There had to be a way to save Sasha.

Sasha had mentioned love.

It was too soon. Right? He thought he'd loved Jonathon and look how that had turned out. But Sasha was different. *They* were different. For such a brutal man, Sasha was incredibly tender. He'd hidden away his softer side. But his art didn't lie.

After years of attending art gallery openings and museum crawls, Viktor appreciated the intimacy and the beauty in Sasha's work.

How hard had it been for him to flatten that empathy and work for the FSB?

And yet, he hadn't lost his sensitivity. He'd just subjugated it.

Viktor wanted time. He needed time. But first he had to convince Sasha that they could make it happen.

Actually, first he needed to find him.

If he hadn't had this paperwork to attend to he would be out the door. They had to get planning.

Jill called him to her office.

"Thanks for coming." She gestured to the chair across from

her desk. Viktor raised his eyebrows. That was awfully formal. She held her body stiffly, as if she were in pain.

"What's up?"

She shifted uncomfortably. "Got notice from the marshals that the girl is settled in a safe house."

"That's good. Until we can figure out what's going on, I think we need to keep her out of the public eye." Two people were dead. He didn't want a third.

Jill was acting weird. But he only marginally noticed.

"Have you called the Cigarette Man?"

"He appears to be out of the office."

"Will you tell me who he works for?"

"The CIA."

"Just like that?"

"It was time."

"Did they say if he was out on official business?" Or was it something more nefarious?

"The response was vague," Jill said. "I've got Kita working on tracking him down." Her face was fierce. "The United States government does not kill people."

Unlike the Russians. But it sure seemed as if the Cigarette Man knew the Russians were killing the witnesses. "I was thinking—"

She interrupted him. "You need to take a break."

"Ah, what?"

"A break," she said it again. Abruptly. "You need to take a break."

He'd told Jill everything about Sasha that he could share. She knew that Sasha was in danger from his own government.

"But we're in the middle of this situation. I can't just abandon him." Sasha needed Viktor whether he'd admit it or not. He couldn't leave Sasha out in the cold. Wasn't that what the Russians were doing to him?

"I know but I don't think…"

"I'm in love with him."

Jill winced. "That's a terrible idea."

It wasn't an idea. It was his life. And it was how he felt. Jill had found her happily ever after. "Am I not allowed to love someone?"

Her face turned white. "Of course you are. It's what I want for you. But Sasha Loblaw is going to hurt you."

"Sasha would never intentionally hurt me."

"Sometimes we don't know people as well as we think we do" she said softly, slowly, her voice heavy with some emotion he couldn't identify.

"Then why not allow me to continue working on this?" It was what drove him. He woke up at night considering different scenarios and trying to come up with answers to why this was happening and how he could save Sasha.

"You're too close to the situation and you aren't thinking properly," Jill replied.

"Like you weren't thinking properly when you hooked up with Hamish?"

She winced again. "Good point."

"I don't want to take a break." Panic welled up inside him, threatening to bowl over him like a rogue wave on the shore.

"It wasn't a request." Her voice was firm.

He fell back against the chair, his body loose and boneless as he realized she wasn't going to back down on this. "But what about the Russians?"

"They've been killing people for years with near impunity. We are not going to be able to change that." She was shaking her head.

"So we should just…give up?" He didn't understand what was happening here. Why was she acting this way? She'd been a passionate defender of justice and protecting those who were in danger from the forces after them.

"We don't have a choice. My loyalty is to *you*. Not anyone else."

"Is it because he was an assassin?" Viktor's anger began to bubble. For the past few years, he'd done everything asked of him. Everything. He'd supported everyone at ALIAS. But now that he needed something for his lover, it was not to be done? A rage rose up inside him cresting like a monster wave. "He doesn't deserve saving?"

"Viktor. That isn't it at all," Jill said. "You should calm down."

"I don't want to calm down." His voice was louder than he expected, booming around her office like explosions from an IED. "I'm asking for help and you—"

The door burst open. "What's going on here?" Jake filled the doorway, his head twisting, searching for the threat. His gaze finally settled on Viktor.

"Everything is fine." Jill's smile was strained.

"It is not fine." Viktor stomped toward freedom. "Nothing is fine."

She was abandoning him. After everything he'd done for ALIAS, for her.

"I'm sorry." Jill's voice was soft, entreating. Her eyes shimmered with tears.

"Me too." He shouldered past Jake and out the door.

What the fuck?

Chapter 17

$\mathcal{I}$t was almost time.

Sasha wanted to say goodbye. He knew it was a mistake, but he called Viktor anyway, unable to help himself. He pressed the speed dial on his burner phone with his right hand. His left hand throbbed, the immense pain nearly overwhelming. He waited as the phone rang.

Physical pain was no match for the devastating despair that shrouded him. A lesser man would be hunched over in agony. But he knew this was the only path.

Viktor finally answered. "Hello."

Sasha could hear the sadness in his voice. "It's me."

"I've been trying to get ahold of you for hours."

"I know." Every time Viktor had called, it had killed Sasha to press decline.

"I am working on a solution." Viktor's voice cracked. "But I am having to do it without my backup."

Panic edged out the pain. "No. Don't trouble yourself." This wasn't in his plan.

"I will find a way to help you."

"I am beyond help."

"No one is beyond help. My friends have taught me this."

No, no, no. "It's fine." He kept his voice even.

"Nothing is fine."

Sasha thought about the past few weeks. "Being with you has been one of the highlights of my life."

"Why does this sound like goodbye?"

"You are a good man, Viktor." Sasha's heart was breaking.

"You're scaring me."

"My time is not long. They will find me, and it will be over."

He'd driven his car today so they could find him, then he'd parked in the garage of his decoy apartment. He wanted this over with. "You have been a great joy."

"I don't like this past tense, Sasha."

"Take care of yourself, *moy lyubimyy*." His beloved. "I have left instructions for you to have my real apartment and anything you want inside it. Do not go to the other one. It is booby-trapped."

"No, wait!" Viktor cried. "I don't want your apartment."

"Then sell it and give the proceeds away to your homeless shelter."

Viktor said, "I am on my way to you."

No! He had to leave now. "Live for me."

Sasha didn't want him pining. He wanted him to have a full life, even if a part of him wanted to eviscerate any man who touched his love.

"You are not going to die," Viktor said fiercely.

"I will not let them use you against me." Sasha touched his finger to his lips and then pressed it against the screen. "Goodbye."

Sasha ended the call, surprised by the wetness on his face. He was not a sentimental man. But Viktor brought out all the emotions in him.

He looked around his decoy apartment. He'd left little surprises for whoever came to clean it out. He should perhaps feel bad since they were just following orders. But they'd attempted to kill him several times over the past week for having the audacity to want to quit this life.

He double-checked one more time, making sure there was nothing that would tie this place to his actual apartment. He had lived a transient life. Always coming and going at the whims of his employers. He did not care for things. He would rather have Viktor.

But dreaming of a life with Viktor was for romantics and fools. And he was a realist.

It was time.

He carried the bag with his misdirection inside it and made one last call. He dialed the ambassador on his private line using his FSB official cell phone. The man picked up right away. Even though it was a private line, Sasha knew that Dubov would be tracking him.

"*Allo.*"

"Sir," Sasha said.

"What have you done?"

"You killed the bartender who drugged me." Sasha wanted confirmation. He locked his front door for the last time and headed outside.

"Da."

"Why are you setting me up?"

"I cannot afford to anger the Kremlin," Dubov hissed. "I have no choice. They want you silenced."

"Why?"

"They do not believe you are sufficiently loyal, and now that your mother is gone, you know too much. Indulging in your lifestyle was the last straw."

So they didn't know he had given information to the

Americans. Good. Dubov would be even more upset when the US authorities challenged him about the assassinations Sasha had carried out. Sasha had given Jillian Larsen a thumb drive with intelligence to pass along to his handler through her contacts.

"My lifestyle?" he said angrily. "I had no life."

"You have been in touch with Viktor Kuznets."

Someone following him must have seen him with Viktor. Fuck.

"I am not going lightly." Because he might be done with killing, but he wasn't about to lie down and die because the FSB had decided that he outlived his usefulness.

"If I don't do what they ask, I will be called back to Moscow and my son will not survive there. You of all people should understand that," Dubov sputtered. "Do not hurt my family."

Because that was the Russian way. If you didn't fall in line, your whole family was in danger. Scorched earth devastation was their policy.

Sasha demanded, "You will not retaliate against Viktor Kuznets. I have plans and safeguards in place in case you succeed in killing me. But I will protect him with everything I have."

"I cannot afford to care what happens to you." Dubov hesitated. "I *am* sorry. You have served me well." He cut the line.

Sasha checked out how long the call had lasted. Good. They had his position.

He took the stairs, not even considering the elevator. When he reached the ground floor, he cautiously exited. His heart thumped in a hard rhythm. Viktor was coming in the lobby of his decoy building.

No!

This was what he'd been trying to avoid.

He should never have called him. His lover was smart. He'd have been tracking him just like his employer. But based on how fast he got here, Sasha had not been thinking clearly. Viktor must have been close by.

He scurried toward the garage, hoping Viktor hadn't seen him. Quickly, he scanned his card for entry.

No one lurked in the corners ready to shoot him down. That was typically not how the FSB operated, but he was taking no chances.

He hustled to his car. He had parked as far away from the elevators as possible, and no one was parked near him. He'd timed this so that most of the building's inhabitants would be at work, and as long as no one was nearby, people should be safe. But there were always factors outside of his control.

He hadn't been this afraid since his first assassination all those years ago. Fearing discovery around every corner. Jumping at every little sound.

He ducked down and saw the bomb attached to the undercarriage of his vehicle.

After opening his car door, he tossed in the bag. He turned off both his official cell phone and the burner he'd used to talk to Viktor. His hand trembled as he placed them on the dashboard.

He bent in and inserted his keys in the ignition.

He studied the car, looking at the suitcase full of his clothes and his passports and his identification in the back seat, and wondering if maybe he should just get in and start it. Maybe this was how it should end. Maybe his whole life had been moving toward this moment.

Maybe he didn't deserve to live anymore.

He'd done terrible things. To some people who didn't deserve it.

While his targets had frequently been criminals, not all of them were bad people. Some were just regular people who'd dared to stand up to Putin and the FSB. Who'd dared to demand a better life for Russian citizens. Was he really deserving of a second chance?

He thought not.

The attack came out of nowhere. Sasha had been so lost in his regrets that he'd been lax in staying on guard.

"Explosion is too easy. You deserve to know you are going to die." Dmitri Kamarov punched Sasha in the side where he'd been stabbed.

Pain burst in his body as he fought with his very soul.

He struck out with hard, heavy punches against the man he'd trained. The fight was brutal, intense.

"You screwed me over." Dmitri complained while they circled each other.

"You screwed yourself by leaving your signature all over her."

"You didn't have to tell the FSB."

The Kremlin did not like surprises. That was what Dmitri had never understood.

"Da. I did. I have no loyalty to you."

Dmitri whipped out an ice pick. One of his favorite weapons. "You are no match for my steel."

This was what Dmitri never understood and what Sasha had tried to impart to Viktor. "My weapon is superior to yours."

Dmitri laughed harshly. "You have no weapon." He jabbed the pick at Sasha's heart.

Shit. Sasha did not have time for this! His mental clock was ticking down the seconds.

"I have my brain." And he struck.

* * *

*V*iktor raced up the stairs to Sasha's apartment. He had skimped on precautions because he hadn't liked the way Sasha had been talking. His life was in shambles. He'd been kicked out of work. Jill had said it was temporary, but that was before he yelled at her.

Now Sasha was making noises as if he were leaving. Or worse, dying.

He needed to talk to him. To touch him and reassure himself that Sasha was here, and he was real.

When he got to the apartment, he started to pull out his universal key. But then Sasha's comments came back to him. He'd booby-trapped it.

He knew Sasha had been here recently because Viktor had tagged his burner phone at the office last night. When Sasha had called him, he'd been at this apartment. The decoy. Not the one where he really lived.

Why would he be at his decoy apartment?

Unless he was trying to get caught. Viktor stood staring at the door. Where would Sasha go next if he were trying to draw attention? His car?

Panic beat at him. Viktor had to find him. To stop him. They could figure this out. They could do anything together.

Viktor headed to the garage to see if Sasha's car was there. He knew Sasha had one, but he rarely used it. As he'd said, tracking his car was too easy. If he wanted to be anonymous or travel without revealing his destination, he used the public transit system. But if he wanted to be found, it made sense to use his car. He was taunting the assassins after him.

Viktor had used GPS to track Sasha's phone, but when he tried to locate him now, the signal was not there. He ran down the stairwell, heading to the parking structure.

He burst into the garage. Sasha's car, the gray Ford Taurus he'd hypothesized about when they first met, was in the far corner. He could see the shadow of a person in the driver's seat.

Viktor started running. "Wait!"

Boom!

The blast threw Viktor off his feet, tossing him backwards. The flames whooshed as the bomb sucked the oxygen in and fed the ultra-hot, chemically induced fire.

Another explosion rocked the garage.

Viktor hit the side of an SUV and slumped to the ground.

Sasha!

Debris fluttered through the air like confetti, multiple car alarms blared, creating a cacophony of sound, and acrid smoke burned his nostrils.

He had to get to Sasha.

Save him, save him echoed in his head like an urgent drumbeat. Fear pounded in his heart and churned in his gut.

Save Sasha.

Viktor staggered to his feet. He'd been far enough away that he'd escaped the heat from the blast, but the percussion had fucked up his eardrums.

His throat hurt. That was when he realized that he was screaming, the muscles in his neck straining.

He tried to run toward Sasha, bouncing off the parked cars like a pinball, staggering from left to right, as he corrected and kept going.

The car was burning; a husk of the frame was all that was left.

He had to get to Sasha.

"Got to get to Sasha." He loped toward the engulfed car.

From the side, someone tackled him.

"Sasha!"

"Vik, my man. You can't go any closer." Jake wrapped his burly arms around Viktor, holding him back.

"Got to save him."

"No one in that car survived." Jake pushed him away, back toward the building. "We need to get out of here."

"Got to save him." Viktor struggled against Jake's hold. "Sasha!"

"He's gone, Vik."

His chest hurt, sorrow squeezing his heart. He breathed in the harsh smoke-filled air, burning his throat. Lost, bereft, forlorn. Wet warmth trailed over his cheeks. "He's gone?"

"Yeah, man." Jake curled his arm around his shoulders, leading him to the exit. "He's gone."

Jake held Viktor up with one arm and dialed his phone with the other. "There's been an explosion." He rattled off the address as he led Viktor outside.

Viktor slumped against Jake, as if all the fight and life had gone out of his body when that car exploded.

His brain was trying to process, make connections, but he felt as if he were swimming through a thick, soupy fog, unable to see anything but what was right in front of him. "What are you doing here?" he said dully.

He kept returning to that moment when the car exploded.

"What...*are* you doing here?" Suddenly his foggy brain clicked into hyper focus.

"Jill asked me to keep an eye on you."

Because she didn't trust him?

Jake said, "She's worried about you."

Viktor tried to drum up some concern, but nothing seemed to matter right now.

"I was following you."

That didn't really seem to make sense. Viktor was careful

even when he skimped on precautions. Yes, he'd been in a hurry to get to Sasha, but he hadn't been completely negligent.

Viktor frowned. "You are good."

"The best, my man."

"Sasha." Viktor stared back toward the garage.

"I'm sorry."

Chapter 18

Viktor stood at Sasha's gravesite.

He'd decided to honor him as best he could. There was not enough of Sasha's body left for three days of mourning. No head to adorn with crowns.

Viktor was numb from the tips of his toes to the ends of his hair. He felt as if he were wading through mud in basic training, slogging and trying to push forward but moving so slowly that progress was difficult.

Most of the time he wondered if he even he wanted to progress.

He'd paid for a gravestone, but no casket because not much of Sasha was left. What was recovered had been cremated.

Viktor held down bile, his stomach revolting at the thought.

Two people had died in the explosion. Sasha and Dmitri Kamarov.

Sasha had been identified through body parts—they found some of his fingers. And they had matched his fingerprints to those supplied by the Russian embassy. Kamarov was identified through his partially burned torso.

The ambassador had vowed to get to the bottom of the car bombing and find justice for his comrades and retribution for their killer, reciting a fiery speech on TV. Viktor thought the man was lying through his teeth.

There was no coffin to circle. But Viktor laid flowers on the headstone, as the priest intoned, "Give thanks to the Lord, for He is good; His love endures forever."

The priest sprinkled soil and holy water over the gravestone. These rituals were designed to bring comfort to the mourners, but Viktor was beyond comfort.

He couldn't even cry. It was as if his soul shriveled up into a husk that would blow away in the frigid January wind.

Jill stood beside him.

"Did I cause this?" Viktor was heartbroken. His grief pulsed, buzzing through his body with random bursts of intensity.

Jake flanked his other side. "His lifestyle, his choices, caused this."

"He was forced into his life. He just wanted to escape."

"There is no escape from the FSB and the Kremlin," Jill said softly. "Only death."

"He was an extraordinary man," Viktor lamented.

Jake wrapped his arm around Viktor's shoulders. "Let him go."

If only it were that easy.

"Come on, bro." Jake led him away. "Let's go home."

"I think I am going to walk." Viktor couldn't stand to be cooped up in a car.

"It's miles to your apartment."

But it was only a mile to Sasha's secret apartment. Right now, Viktor needed to be close to him. "You go on ahead."

Jill and Jake left, reluctantly. But it was fine. Viktor wanted to be alone. Needed time to grieve.

The Cigarette Man sidled up to the gravesite in a new disguise. A rounded belly, ill-fitting suit, some sort of padding in his cheeks, thinning hair mostly covered by a beanie. But he was still wearing that stupid scuffed shoe. What the fuck was he doing here?

Viktor still didn't know his name, but he knew that he worked for the CIA. Jill had given him that much. She'd tried to find a way to implicate the man, but they hadn't been able to prove that he had anything to do with either the sex worker or the bartender's death. Even though the other sex worker had identified him as the man who paid them to entrap Viktor and Sasha, there was no paper trail that lead to him. Viktor had the photos on his phone, but that was the only remnant of his supposed op.

They had searched repeatedly for any way to connect him to the murders. Viktor knew the man was dirty, but they had no evidence.

"Did you set this up?" Could Cigarette Man somehow have caused Sasha's death?

"Of course not." Cigarette Man stared at the giant wreath of flowers. "He really is dead?"

Viktor wanted to punch the man. Viktor was sure he was working with the Russians. So what was he doing here, out in the open?

"Yes. He fucking blew up." Probably because of this man.

"Unfortunate. I was looking forward to the intelligence he had."

Viktor's eyes burned, rimmed with red and dry because he hadn't been able to sleep. Every time he shut his eyes, he saw Sasha's car explode over and over again like a movie stuck on auto replay.

"Why?" Viktor asked dully. Why had this man imploded Sasha's life?

"I wanted to prove to the brass that I was worthy of promotion. I've been passed over several times. I just thought if I could bag Loblaw, I'd get some respect."

There was something in his voice that Viktor needed to pay attention to. But Viktor was too intent on turning the screws, wanting to hurt this man the way he had hurt him.

The man dug his toe against the hard, frozen ground. That scuff taunted Viktor.

Viktor couldn't ask what he needed to know. Why did he set up Sasha? "What's up with the scuff on your shoe?"

The man shrugged. "Just a reminder to me to…do my best. My boss was in the military, and he isn't a fan of the scuff. He likes things spit shined and picture perfect."

"You wanted to embarrass him?"

"He's a douchebag who doesn't know anything about tradecraft or recruitment."

Viktor read between the lines. He was a disgruntled employee?

"You could really show him by working with the Russians."

The man jerked. "I would never do that."

"Of course not. That would be treason." Viktor hunched in his jacket. "Punishable by death…or a minimum of five years in prison."

"Exactly." The man clapped his hand on Viktor's shoulder. "That is not what I want."

Viktor shrugged away the hand. "Even worse would be if the Russians found out you were double-crossing them."

The man blanched. "Are you accusing me of something?"

"You were working with the Russians to try and recruit me but against the Russians to use me to recruit Sasha for the US government. I don't think either government would be happy about that."

"Pure conjecture." He rubbed his belly. "And you can't prove it."

A sense of satisfaction surged through him. Sasha might be gone, but his death would not go unavenged. Now he had a reason for living.

The world might be gray—but a burning dark purple rage was flowing through his bones like the slashes of color in Sasha's photos.

He didn't have to have proof...he just needed to reveal the truth to the right people.

* * *

*V*iktor let himself in to Sasha's real apartment. He didn't want to be alone. He had taken the Metro, switching trains and doubling back, making sure he didn't have a tail.

He couldn't help but think that the funeral had been under surveillance. He hadn't seen anyone, but that hyper sense that he'd developed on the street when he'd been a kid had been tingling.

He flattened his palm against the wall where Sasha had pressed up against him. He trailed his fingers along the frames of the photographs, unable to fathom that someone who had lived Sasha's life had been able to capture such intense photographs.

He rummaged through drawers, looking, searching for something, anything that he could take that would remind him of Sasha.

The apartment felt so empty. It had only been a few days, but the air was stale. He studied the small end table next to the sofa. He pulled out the drawer. Nothing but the television remote. He felt inside the cavity, and there was an envelope taped to the underside of the top of the small table.

Viktor ripped the envelope off. *For Viktor. You will never be homeless again,* was written on the outside in Sasha's slashing handwriting and signed only with his name. No flowery script or declarations. Inside was the key for a safe deposit box and the number 527. The note said Viktor would know where to find the box. But he had no idea.

He found a box of vinyl gloves under the sink and pulled them on. Then he went around the apartment, searching the picture frames, lifting the photographs off the wall and checking the backings. A teacup sat in the dish drainer as if Sasha had just stepped out.

Viktor dug through the toiletries in the bathroom, removed the outlet covers, checked the light bulbs. After he meticulously searched the entire apartment, he gave up. He didn't know what Sasha meant.

He didn't need the safety deposit box and its contents. What he needed was Sasha.

Then he looked for Sasha's camera, but he couldn't find it. He crawled between the sheets and clutched a pillow to his chest, breathing in trying to find Sasha's scent. Searching for peace.

He lay his head down and stared at the white walls aching for the life he'd hoped to have. Maybe it was naïve, but he'd thought they could find a way.

What the hell had Sasha been thinking, getting in that car without checking for explosives? It was almost as if he'd wanted to get blown up.

Damn him.

Viktor was dry-eyed as he lay in his lover's bed and mourned for something that could never be.

The next morning, as he was leaving red-eyed and groggy

with lack of sleep, he tidied up and then started to pull the blinds. And that's when he saw it. In the reflection of the mirror, he saw a bank across the street.

He'd check out the safety deposit box and donate whatever was inside.

* * *

Viktor walked to his apartment. The bitter cold whistled through his jacket, chilling his bones. He hadn't been in a car since the explosion.

He was almost home when a diplomatic limousine rolled up next to him, then pulled slightly ahead and stopped.

Viktor hunched into the warmth of his jacket and kept on walking.

The window rolled down. "Mr. Kuznets."

"Not interested."

"Get in." A bulky Russian bodyguard stood in front of him, blocking his path.

He had nothing to lose.

He slid into the limo and stared sullenly at the man who likely gave the order to kill Sasha.

"I have a proposition for you." Ambassador Dubov didn't look evil, but Viktor knew that his smooth exterior hid a dangerous man. "I'd like you to gather information for me."

"Not interested."

"You are not seeming to understand your position."

"I understand just fine." Viktor said, "You set me up so you could compromise me and blackmail me to work for you. But I love my country: America. And I will not betray her."

"Blackmail is such an ugly word."

Viktor shrugged. "Call it whatever you want. Not interested."

"We have information regarding the unfortunate death of a woman you are acquainted with."

Viktor waited.

"The murder weapon has been found. I believe you will recognize it." He pulled up a picture of Viktor's tactical baton.

Viktor rolled his eyes. "I don't care."

"I can make the whole thing go away," Dubov said silkily.

"I don't care." Viktor reiterated. "You killed the only leverage that mattered."

"He really is dead." Dubov sounded a bit shocked. "He hasn't touched his bank accounts since that day. There's been no sighting of him."

The slight hope that maybe somehow Sasha was still alive withered and died. "I watched him blow up." Viktor swallowed convulsively.

Dubov waited silently. "You are alive. And in some trouble."

"I'd be happy to explain that I was drugged, and that the woman's death had the figurative fingerprints of your dead assassin all over it.

"I am not going to change your mind." Dubov raised a brow, tilting his head as if he were studying a particularly fascinating animal.

"Nope."

"You loved him that much?"

"Yes." He was heartbroken. The ambassador was untouchable. But he had one ace to play. "I know I can't get you. I know that you have diplomatic immunity. But…"

The ambassador leaned forward.

Viktor said, "I have something for you. In exchange for leaving me alone."

The ambassador pressed a button on the door handle and

the window between the driver and the backseat raised. "We can talk freely."

"You were looking for a traitor. A double agent?"

"Da." Now Dubov looked confused. Viktor could see the truth dawn in his eyes as he realized that Sasha had talked to Viktor about this.

Viktor open an app on his phone and pulled up the picture of the Cigarette Man. When Sasha had been in the ALIAS office, Sasha had transferred the pictures outside the motel to the Adams-Larsen computers. "He is your double agent."

"I don't know him." But his eyelids flickered, and Viktor knew he was lying.

"You lie," Viktor said. "But I don't care."

"What makes you think he's a double agent?"

"He blackmailed me to compromise Sasha. He was trying to convert him to spy for the CIA." Viktor left out the part where Sasha had already been spying for the US. "We're even now. Don't bother me again."

The ambassador's mouth tightened. "Why would you tell me this?"

"Because he helped you kill Sasha." Viktor reached for the door handle. "While I consider myself an American, I am Russian enough to want revenge."

Chapter 19

*O*ne *month later*
Viktor read the *Washington Post* while he rode the Metro into work. Several pages in, there was a small box about the sudden heart attack death of a homeless man at a train station. And on another page, an article about how Russia had recalled their ambassador.

He trudged into the office, avoiding the conference room where he could hear everyone getting ready for their Monday morning staff meeting. Their banter was like nails on a chalkboard, an irritant rather than the pleasure it used to be.

Jill called his cell and he figured she was summoning him to the meeting. Instead, she said, "Viktor, can you come to my office?" He headed into Jill's office. He hadn't been performing up to the right standards. He tried to care but nothing really seemed to matter.

"Come on in." She gestured to the chairs. "Have a seat."

"What do you need?" His response was lackluster.

"It's not what I need. You need a vacation."

"No, I don't." He shook his head. The last time she'd insisted he needed a break, his lover had died.

"I insist."

He frowned.

"I booked you a cabin in Maine." Jillian pulled a burner phone and a folio with a wad of cash and a pre-loaded Visa card. "I took care of everything."

Jake walked in the office. "I'll take you to the airport."

"I don't want to go."

"You need a break, man."

Finally, Viktor acquiesced. He left with a backpack filled with one flannel shirt and the important contents of Sasha's safety deposit box. A letter and picture of a cottage by the sea. *I had hoped one day to share that cottage with you. Dream of me always.*

Viktor fumed the entire way to Maine. He didn't want to be away. Maybe he hadn't been at his best recently, but he'd shown up every day and put in the hours, trying desperately to forget the few weeks that had changed his life.

But around every corner was a fresh memory.

Maybe they were right. Maybe he just needed to get out of DC. Away from the memories. Away from the grief.

Hours later, the taxi dropped Viktor off at a tiny cabin, barely larger than a hotel room. Rustic logs formed the walls, a small sofa and coffee table filled the living area, and a long counter with a fridge, microwave, coffee pot, and sink comprised the kitchen. As soon as he arrived, he fell into the double bed with the old-fashioned quilt on top.

The next morning, he awoke early and found an envelope on the desk in the living room that he'd missed last night. Inside were keys to a car —with Canadian plates and a full tank of gas—stored in the shed behind the cabin, and an old-fashioned paper map highlighting an obscure route into Nova Scotia and onto Cape Breton Island. The road in was remote and unmonitored by border patrol. No passport needed.

These were tactics they used to relocate their clients.

Viktor was confused. Intrigued. More than he had been in months.

The clues had awoken something inside him, and he got on the road. Twelve hours later, he began the drive around Cape Breton on the Cabot Trail. He drove slowly through the towns and villages, wondering what he was looking for. The area was rural and deserted compared to the bustle of the streets of the District of Columbia.

He pulled into a small restaurant on the side of the road. The bright red sign promised fish and chips and a chilled beer. After his filling dinner, he wandered the small village, still confused about what he was looking for.

The route on the map couldn't be random.

Dusk was coming and he'd need a place to stay. This town seemed as good as any. Viktor passed an art gallery with a window display of black-and-white photographs doctored with slashes of color. One photo in particular caught his eye, a moody landscape of the clouds and the crash of waves on the rocky shore and slash of deep, cerulean blue.

Viktor stopped short. It reminded him of Sasha. He barreled into the shop.

An older white man sat in a chair by the sales counter. "Can I help you?"

"The photo in the window." Viktor's heart was beating so hard he was lightheaded.

"Isn't it wonderful?" the shopkeeper gushed. "So evocative."

"What is the artist's name?"

"He's local. Laurent Agard."

Local. Viktor deflated. Of course it wasn't Sasha. How could he even for a minute have thought Sasha was here?

Sasha was dead.

"His work reminds me of someone I used to know."

And just like that, Viktor was sad again.

"He's very reclusive." The shopkeeper leaned closer. "I think it's probably because of his accident."

Viktor paused. "What happened?"

"Not sure exactly but he's missing several fingers on his left hand and he's got some scars."

Viktor looked at the photograph again. On the bottom right, the signature was a bold slash of *LA*. But Viktor recognized that handwriting.

It couldn't be. Could it?

"Do you have contact information for him?"

"I can't give that out. He's very private."

Viktor needed to meet him. To see if it was Sasha. He thought about their dream and that picture that Sasha had left for him in the safety deposit box. Surely it couldn't be. "Are there any seaside cottages nearby?"

"*Mais, oui.*"

The shopkeeper pulled out one of those cartoon type maps that showcased businesses where nothing was to scale. He circled an area not too far from the shop and told him to follow the road and he'd see the signs. Darkness had fallen. There was no way to continue tonight. Impatience jittered through Viktor.

Could Sasha be alive?

* * *

*V*iktor had found a small B&B to crash last night. This morning, he leapt out of bed, grabbed the map, and headed out.

Then he had an idea. He retrieved the picture Sasha had left him in the safety deposit box from his backpack and ran back into the small hotel. He asked the older white woman who ran the front desk of the bed and breakfast, "Is there any place like this around?"

The cottage showed the sea in the background. A curved brick walkway led to an arched wood front door with a wrought iron knocker and a small window set high in the wood.

Clusters of rose bushes lined the walkway and hugged the house. Window boxes overflowing with flowers sat beneath tall narrow windows like a smile. A chimney perched on one end of the roof. Dormer windows looked out over the ocean.

"Sure is." She smiled widely, showing a mouthful of slightly crooked teeth. "That looks like the old crofter's cottage on St. Margaret's Lane."

Viktor followed the woman's directions, his heart beating in triple time.

For the first time in months, he had hope.

He drove for an hour, almost about to give up. The winding road was beautiful, the ocean to his left, as he scoured the somewhat hidden cottages looking for *the* one.

He hadn't seen a car in kilometers. Suddenly he came around the bend and there it was.

Viktor pulled into the overgrown driveway. A bike with a basket on the front was propped against the side of the garage, and a puff of smoke from the chimney rose into the air.

He pulled the picture from the dash with trembling hands.

He exited the car, his whole body shaking as adrenaline coursed through him. His heart wanted to burst right out of his chest. He took a deep breath and tried to quell his galloping heart.

This was it.

* * *

*L*aurent Agard heard the car pull into the drive. He'd anticipated this moment since he'd gotten a call last night. He waited in the small parlor, the heat from the fire warming him. He was cold. So cold.

Because the next few minutes would determine his life.

Whether he lived alone and lonely, or whether he had a chance at a new beginning.

The knock at the door was bold and unapologetic.

He opened the door and hungrily stared at Viktor.

"Bonjour." His voice was rough, with a gravelly texture from vocal cords damaged by the heat of the fire. He'd detonated the bomb while he was closer than he'd have preferred. But he couldn't afford to wait because Viktor had been headed toward the car.

Viktor stood still, staring at him, not coming inside. He knew he looked different. "Mr. Agard?"

The plastic surgeon had done things to his nose and his jaw, sculpting it away to reveal a different face. "*Oui. Je m'appelle Laurent Agard.*" Every time he said his new name it got easier.

He couldn't help it. He reached toward his lover, hoping that he wouldn't reject him. So desperate to touch him, to rejoice in the fact that he was finally here.

But Viktor stepped back.

Laurent's heart nearly broke.

Until Viktor whispered, "Are those your photographs at the gallery?"

"*Oui.*"

Viktor stepped inside and but left the door open. "I am in love with them."

His heart thumped hard at the word *love*.

"*Merci.* I thought of my lover as I took them." He held up

his left hand and showed the ragged edges where he'd cut off his fingers. They had needed his DNA to be found at the blast site and losing them was a small price to pay, but what if Viktor rejected the new him? He didn't look like himself, he didn't sound like himself. "I have some…defects."

Viktor studied his hand, and then lifted his gaze to his new blue eyes. "What happened?"

"Factory accident." Laurent shrugged in a very Gallic way. "*C'est la vie.*"

"I'm sorry," Viktor said.

"I'm not. It brought me here." To this new life.

"I like it here. Do you have room for another?"

Relief cascaded through him. "I would like that very much."

Everything in his life had brought him to this moment. All the pain and heartache of the past few months disintegrated. The redemption and reward for his life was about to become reality.

Once the door closed, Viktor launched himself at Laurent.

They crashed together in a torrent of passion, hard kisses, tender sighs, hugging each other tightly. "It *is* you." Viktor knew not to say his old name out loud.

"*Oui.*" Passion overwhelmed him. Love, gratitude swelled through him. They needed to talk. They needed to plan. He prayed that this was not just a short visit. If Viktor decided to leave, Laurent would have to move.

Viktor pushed him up against the front door and devoured his mouth. "The hooked rug. The fire."

He ripped the tight blue polo shirt over his head, then tugged at Viktor's shirt. "*Oui,*" he said with breathless anticipation.

Viktor's fingers tore at the button on his jeans. "You were waiting for me?"

"*Oui.*" He shoved Viktor's jeans down and reached for him.

Viktor tugged him over to the rug and pulled him down to lie beside him.

"It's our dream."

"*Oui.*"

"What's next?"

And Laurent showed him.

* * *

*V*iktor lay on the rug, breathing heavily. His heartbeat thumped in his ears. The fire crackled merrily as they lay on a bed of their clothes.

Sa…Laurent rose lazily and poured two glasses of cognac from a bottle on the small sideboard that held a sampling of French wines and liqueurs. He was thinner, rangier. Viktor took in the small changes in his body, cataloguing the new.

Laurent sank down in front of the fire.

"*A ta santé.*" The clink of glasses topped off the hushed atmosphere.

"Can you tell me?"

"Once, and then we must never speak of it again."

Viktor watched the firelight flicker over his lover's face, highlighting the sculpted cheekbones and jawline of a different man. "How?"

"Your boss helped me. She drove me away in her trunk."

Certain things from that day came back to Viktor. He hadn't been thinking straight or he would have realized that Jake being there didn't make sense. "Jake wasn't following me?"

"*Non.* We didn't plan on you coming to the building." He

brushed his hand over Viktor's hair. "I was so scared that you would be hurt. I insisted that he take care of you."

"What happened next?"

"Your boss is an extraordinary woman."

"I told you," Viktor said smugly.

"She got me to a plastic surgeon and they," he gestured to his face with a grimace. "Changed me."

Viktor grabbed the disfigured hand. "You cut off your fingers."

"They needed to find my DNA." That had cemented his death and convinced the FSB and the Russians to stop looking for him.

Viktor scrolled through everything that had happened since Sasha's car had blown up. "How did you know I was coming?"

"Prearranged signal on a burner phone that is now in pieces at the local dump."

Viktor was silent.

"What happened with you after I…left?"

"The ambassador approached to try to coerce me to work for them."

"*Merde.* I knew it." He threaded their fingers together. "How did you escape?"

"I placated him."

"How?"

"I gave him the traitor."

"No one ever knew it was…." A grimace pulled at Laurent's face.

"Nope," Viktor said. "Cigarette Man is dead. He was the double agent."

"How?"

"Ruled a heart attack."

"Ah, poisoned." Laurent nodded. "Not a surprise."

Viktor refused to feel bad about his death. "Let us not speak of death anymore." He set his cognac on the coffee table.

"What would you like to speak about then?" Laurent set his glass down and leaned in for a tender kiss.

"Life. I would like to speak about life."

"Together?" Laurent asked.

"Together." Viktor wrapped his arms around his future and said a mental goodbye to the past. Finally, he found where he belonged.

In this man's arms.

***

What is up with Jake? Click here to pre-order Conned (ALIAS #6), the final book in the ALIAS series.

I'm also offering Duped (An ALIAS Prequel) for free through Bookfunnel. Click here to download. <3

*I*f you haven't read the rest of the series, start here with Stalked (ALIAS #1), an opposites attract, have to work together romantic suspense.

Thank you for reading Viktor and Sasha!

Thank you for reading Viktor and Sasha's love story!

Also by Lisa Hughey

<u>ALIAS</u>

<u>Duped (An ALIAS Prequel)</u>

Stalked (ALIAS #1)

Hunted (ALIAS #2)

Vanished (ALIAS #3)

Deceived (ALIAS #4)

Saved (ALIAS Short)

Compromised (ALIAS #5)

Conned (ALIAS #6)

<u>Black Cipher Files Romantic Suspense</u>

<u>The Encounter, A Prequel to Blowback</u>

<u>Blowback</u>

<u>Betrayals</u>

<u>Burned</u>

<u>Dangerous Game</u>

<u>Black Cipher Files Box Set (includes Blowback, Betrayals, and Burned)</u>

<u>Snow Creek Christmas</u>

<u>Love on Main Street: A Snow Creek Christmas – 7 Author anthology</u>

<u>One Silent Night</u> (from Love on Main Street)

<u>Miracle on Main Street</u> (standalone novella)

<u>Family Stone Romantic Suspense</u>

<u>Stone Cold Heart, (Jess, Family Stone #1)</u>

<u>Carved in Stone (Connor, Family Stone #2)</u>

<u>Heart of Stone (Riley, Family Stone #3)</u>

<u>Still the One (Jack, Family Stone #4)</u>

<u>Jar of Hearts (Keisha & Shane, Family Stone #5)</u>

<u>Queen of Hearts (Shelley, Family Stone #6)</u>

<u>Cold as Stone (John, Family Stone #7)</u>

<u>Family Stone Box Set (Stone Cold Heart, Carved in Stone, Heart of Stone, Still the One, & Jar of Hearts)</u>

<u>The Nostradamus Prophecies</u>

<u>View To A Kill #1</u>

Never Say Never #2

<u>Billionaire Breakfast Club</u>

His Semi-Charmed Life (Camp Firefly Falls #11 and Billionaire Breakfast Club #0)

Everything He Wants (Billionaire Breakfast Club #1 The Jock)

She Feels Like Home (Billionaire Breakfast Club #3)

About Lisa

USA Today Bestselling Author Lisa Hughey started writing romance in the fourth grade. That particular story involved a prince and an engagement. Now, she writes about strong heroines who are perfectly capable of rescuing themselves and the heroes who love both their strength and their vulnerability. She pens romances of all types—suspense, paranormal, and contemporary—but at their heart, all her books celebrate the power of love.

She lives in Cape Ann Massachusetts with her fabulously supportive husband, and two adorable but skittish tuxedo rescue cats.

Beach walks, hiking, and traveling are her favorite ways to pass the time when she isn't plotting new ways to get her characters to fall in love.

Lisa loves to hear from readers and has tons of places you can connect with her. It's a wonder she gets any writing done at all....

Sign Up for Lisa's Confidants
  Visit Lisa on the Web

Follow Lisa's Boards on Pinterest
Follow Lisa on Instagram
Email Lisa
Be Lisa's Friend on Goodreads
Like Lisa on Facebook at Lisa Hughey: My Books